R

THE
SHELTON
CONSPIRACY

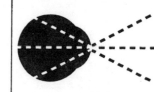

THE
SHELTON
CONSPIRACY

RAE FOLEY

Thorndike Press • Thorndike, Maine

OCT 25 1993

Thorndike Large Print ® Romance Series edition published in 1993 by arrangement with Golden West Literary Agency.

The tree indicium is a trademark of Thorndike Press.

This book is printed on acid-free, high opacity paper.⊚

Set in 16 pt. News Plantin by Minnie B. Raven.

Library of Congress Cataloging in Publication Data

Foley, Rae, 1900–
    The Shelton conspiracy / Rae Foley.
      p. cm.
    ISBN 0-7862-0026-X (alk. paper : lg. print)
    1. Large type books. I. Title.
[PS3507.E5725S5 1993]
813'.54—dc20

                                             93-26720
                                                CIP

THE
SHELTON
CONSPIRACY

ONE

WAR HERO AND WIFE MURDERED

The bodies of Lieutenant Robert Masson and his wife Lillian were found this morning by their housekeeper, Mrs. Helen Cushing. They had been shot to death in their home at Shelton, Connecticut. Apparently they had been dead for some hours. So far no clues to the killer have been revealed by the State Police.

Lieutenant Masson, better known to his countless friends as Robin, was one of the most decorated heroes of the Vietnam war. On his discharge from the army, nine months ago, with multiple injuries, he returned to his boyhood home in the village of Shelton where, five months later, he married Lillian Halsted. A Hero's Corner was created on the Village Green with a plaque to commemorate his brilliant and daring exploits.

Private services will be held on Wednesday at ten o'clock at the First Congregational Church in Shelton. On Thursday evening at eight a memorial service will take place in the Town Hall to which the public is invited. The principal speaker will be Millard Welford.

The only surviving relation is Hall Masson,

brother of the murdered man, historian, lecturer, and author of The Meaning of Freedom and A Faceless Generation. *Efforts to reach Mr. Masson, who is abroad gathering material for a series of articles, have failed.*

The housekeeper, Mrs. Cushing, who discovered the bodies of her employers on her arrival this morning, is said to be in a state of shock and unavailable for questioning.

Captain Gerfind of the State Police stated this morning that the killer would be found. An award of $25,000 has been offered by Bruce Halsted, retired industrialist and resident of Shelton, for any evidence that will lead to the discovery of the killer. Mr. Halsted is the uncle of Mrs. Masson who, before her marriage, was the popular debutante, Lillian Halsted.

The exploits of Lieutenant Masson during his short term of duty in Vietnam have already become legendary. "The intrepid courage of this young man," General Gates remarked when decorating him on the field, "is in the finest tradition of our times. While we have such men as Lieutenant Masson on our side we can be hopeful for the future of America."

Expressions of shock and grief are being heard all over the country. The President has wired his condolences to the people of Shelton. The Governor of Connecticut referred to the double murder as a dastardly outrage. "Today," he said, "not only Shelton but the entire country is in mourning."

II

This news item was three weeks old when Hall Masson found it with a stack of mail and cables awaiting him at his hotel in Cairo.

That night, though he did not appear for dinner, he sent down for a bottle of whisky. Next morning he arranged for the first possible flight home. After a practiced look at the set, gray face, the clerk checked the usual polite expressions of regret at his departure. Something about the American's frozen stillness warned him.

There were cameramen and reporters with microphones at the Kennedy airport when he landed. Only the hardiest dared address the grim-faced man.

"What are your plans, Mr. Masson?"

"I am going to find my brother's killer."

The story was on the air within an hour.

III

In the cramped telephone booth at the library Gail Carlyle dialed a number.

"Greg? Have you heard the news?"

"About Masson, you mean?"

9

"Of course."

"What about it?" In spite of his easy manner Gail sensed her brother's tension.

"Do you think he's going to make trouble?"

Greg gave a bark of laughter. "He's going to try; that's for sure."

"Oh, Greg!"

"Take it easy, kid. There's nothing to worry about."

"Isn't there?" she asked somberly.

IV

The Halsted house was the showplace of Shelton, a big white Colonial on a rise above the Green, set in landscaped grounds. On the annual Garden Tour the public was permitted to see the rooms on the lower floor, rooms that seemed to have been lifted bodily from a museum. But for the most part, except for a small staff, the spacious residence was occupied only by Bruce Halsted and his wife Harriet, who pottered gently around the grounds, listened to their large record collection, and watched over their greenhouses, seeing comparatively few people since the marriage of Halsted's niece, Lillian, to Robert Masson.

Forty years of entertaining for business reasons had provided them with few friends.

After forty years of banquets and speeches they had little desire for public appearances. Halsted was always ready to meet a community need with his checkbook, so long as he was not required to do anything more. His only voluntary public statement since his retirement had followed the discovery of the murders and his offer of a reward.

Mrs. Halsted, so self-effacing as to appear invisible, had long been a cause of wonder to her husband's acquaintances. That a man in his position should be married to so dim a creature surprised everyone. But Harriet Halsted was either unaware of their disdain or indifferent to it. Small, white-haired, unfashionable in dress, she knew that she was as necessary to her husband as he was to her. Either alone would have felt amputated.

She was stretched out on a long chair on the lawn, shaded by three immense elms. Lying neglected on her lap was Edith Hamilton's *Mythology*. An article in *The New York Times* had disturbed her. Too many senior citizens — how she was beginning to loathe that phrase — were neglecting to provide new ideas and stimulus to their minds, with a result that the mind rusted before the muscles lost their elasticity. What was needed was a plunge into new and stimulating fields of interest.

11

Harriet Halsted considered her mental state with detachment. It was true. Aside from music and flowers she had no abiding interests, certainly no new ones. Skimming over the titles on the shelves in the bookroom — Bruce said it was arrogant to call a collection of ten thousand books a library — she had hastily passed the sections on science and philosophy and paused dubiously to open a volume of Greek plays. Dear me, what very unpleasant people they seemed to have been! Her chief impression from her school days was that the Greeks had been involved in slaughtering their own families in the most disagreeable manner. After frowning over a page she put back the book. It wasn't hot weather reading. Perhaps next winter she would try again.

Her hand rested on Edith Hamilton's *Mythology*. Everyone knew that Edith Hamilton had been a remarkable woman. Certainly she hadn't let her brain rust. What one woman could write another woman could read, Harriet told herself but without conviction, and she settled on the lawn in the shade, opening the book with determination. If her mind were to be saved from rust the time was now.

Under a light breeze the leaves of elms and maples scattered over the lawn whispered like rain. Now and then she looked up to see a robin hopping self-importantly over the lawn,

12

cocking his head in disapproval at the grass, which, this dry season, was turning brown. The clear call of a cardinal brought her eyes up in time to see a scarlet streak across the blue sky.

The book dropped in her lap. What a peaceful world! She caught her breath in pain as she thought of Lillian and Robin who had died violently in the little Cape Cod cottage that could be seen through the trees. She squeezed her eyes shut and shook her head. She wouldn't think of it. She must not think of it. But in spite of herself she saw Lillian running across the lawn in her white tennis shorts and shirt, her slim brown legs bare, bright hair glinting in the sunlight. She had always reminded them of Alice in Wonderland.

Harriet remembered Lillian and Robin announcing their engagement, laughing and confident, breathless with plans for their future. And there was no future. Just four months of marriage and now they were dead.

"No," she told herself fiercely. She had determined to put the tragedy behind her for Bruce's sake. Bruce had aged so terribly in the weeks since Lillian had been killed.

The marriage to Robin had been the only thing in which Bruce had ever opposed Lillian's wishes. Probably they had spoiled her but they had had no children of their own.

13

When Bruce's brother died they became the child's guardians. She had been like sunlight in the house.

Bruce had been odd about the engagement. He had told Lillian she was too young. He had said that Robin had been through terrible experiences which she could never share, that he had physical disabilities as a result of his war service, that he couldn't participate in the tennis and skating and dancing she loved.

It was the only time Lillian had ever been angry with her uncle and the white heat of her temper had seared them both, leaving scars. Robin was a hero. He was the man she loved. He was the man she intended to marry.

And she had married him. Looking out at the blue line of hills Harriet remembered the wedding, the radiance of the young couple, unaware of anything but each other, not even disturbed by the presence of reporters and cameramen who had come to record the marriage of the war hero.

Bruce had given away the bride. Whatever objection he had felt to the marriage he never referred to it again. The young Massons had settled in the house Robin's aunt had left him, along with her small fortune of three hundred thousand dollars. "My older nephew, Hall, has already received his fair share of my estate," she had written austerely.

It was only on the last day of Lillian's life that Harriet became aware that something was wrong. That day Bruce had sent for his niece. This time it was he who betrayed a hitherto unexpected temper that erupted like a volcano. Lillian had slammed out of the house screaming, "You have no right! You'll be sorry!"

Next morning she and Robin had been found dead. And that same day the letter had come.

Harriet removed her glasses and wiped her eyes. She blew her nose. She was not going to think of it. She picked up the book and forced her mind to follow the words she was reading:

". . . the Erinyes (the Furies) . . . Their office was to pursue and punish sinners. They were called 'those who walk in darkness,' and they were terrible of aspect, with writhing snakes for hair and eyes that wept tears of blood."

Harriet closed the book and dropped it on the table beside her chair. She switched on a small transistor radio and sat bolt upright as she heard a voice ask, "What are your plans, Mr. Masson?"

"I am going to find my brother's killer."

As Harriet cried out, the gardener looked up from the rose bush he was spraying and

15

ran to the greenhouse. A moment later Bruce Halsted came quickly toward his wife.

"Harriet! What's wrong?"

"Bruce," she choked. "Oh, Bruce!" For the first time in her life she fainted.

V

Millard Welford pulled in at Harry's Service Station. That was his wife's idea. Freda was as wide awake as they come.

"Use them all in turn," she advised him. "Don't give your business to just one outfit."

He reached over to squeeze her knee. No doubt about it, Freda always knew the score. A year ago she had been a platinum blonde with a beehive hair-do and dresses cut way down to there. Now, as the wife of a coming politician, her hair had gone back to its original brown, she went easy on the makeup, and her simply cut summer dress was neither too far above the knee nor too low at the neck. With a wife like Freda a man could go far.

"Hi, Harry, how's the boy?" As a candidate for Congress, Millard was learning fast that every vote counts. "Hot enough for you?"

Harry grinned lopsidedly as the result of a skin graft, a shell having removed part of his face in Vietnam. "Morning, Congressman."

Millard laughed. "Not yet. Got to get those names on the petition first."

"Maybe when you're elected you can get rid of that heap."

"You talking about my old covered wagon?" Millard asked in mock indignation. Always go along with a gag. People are distrustful of public officials who are more intelligent than they are. Look what happened to Adlai Stevenson. "It's practically a member of my family."

"Feels like a member of my family, too," Harry said. "I've sat up nights with this junk pile trying to keep it running for you." He started to polish the windshield. "I guess Masson's death was a blow to you. Old friends and all that."

Millard had to turn his head to look at him as his left eye was glass. A good job, Harry thought; only now and then when the light was just right you really noticed it. Aside from that one defect Millard Welford looked like a combination of Superman and an all-American football star, not much forehead but a lot of jaw. Inspired confidence in people who were used to television programs. He was their sort of man.

"I'll miss him," Millard said heavily. "Known him since I was in my last year at college and he was a freshman."

"He never finished, did he?"

17

"Well, you know how Robin was. He wanted firsthand living and he couldn't find that in books."

"I'm sure sorry for you. Having him back you was powerful stuff. America's hero. That practically put it in the bag for you." Through the windshield Harry watched Millard's hands tighten on the wheel.

A horn sounded and the man in the Chevrolet on the other side of the pumps called, "Hey, Buddy, can you tell me how to find the Masson house?"

Harry turned slowly, the fingers of one hand unconsciously covering the scarred lips. "No one there now. Hadn't you heard? They had a double murder in the house."

"Someone should be there. Hall Masson, the brother, has come back." The man held out a card. *"Daily Chronicle. I'm looking for a story."*

"I can't help you. No one told me he was coming. Your guess is as good as mine as to why he's come back."

"Oh, I know why," the reporter said. "He is looking for his brother's killer."

"If he's smart," Harry said, "he'll go back where he came from. Shelton can solve its own murders."

"Then why doesn't it?" the reporter inquired. "What's that address?"

"It's the Cape Cod at the top of the Green. There's a big white Colonial in the center; a modern house, barn red, on the right; the Cape Cod is on the left. You can't miss it."

As the reporter sketched a salute and put his car in gear, Harry turned to Millard. "So the New York press — what's left of it — is going to take an interest in the Masson murders in picturesque Shelton. Ought to be an interesting summer." His mouth twisted in a smile. "I'm afraid that will distract some attention from your campaign, Congressman."

"Go to hell!" In his haste Millard stalled his car and he heard Harry laugh as he went back to the garage.

VI

Harry stood watching the repair work being done by his three young helpers, offered advice to one, spoke sharply to a second, nodded to the third. Then he went into his office and sat down in a swivel chair. The room wasn't more than eight feet square but it was his. He leaned back in the chair and put his feet on the desk.

"Congressman," he said and laughed aloud. He broke off as one of his helpers came in. "Yeah, Jake?"

"You give me that Harris job and promised

19

it for tonight." His voice was already beginning to take on an aggrieved whine.

"So what?"

"This is Wednesday."

"So it's Wednesday. We don't repair cars on Wednesday?"

"I report to old Burgess Wednesday afternoons."

"Okay, okay, we got to play along with that. I'll put someone else on the Harris job. How you making out with Burgess? Is the old man still keeping tabs on you?"

"That's what he thinks. Until September." Jake snorted. "Unless he forgets. It's like having a nursemaid, only if he was a nursemaid he'd forget where he left the baby."

"Better than having a record," Harry warned him. "I made that clear in the beginning. You get a record and you're out. Anyhow, Burgess is harmless. He was still teaching history when I was in high school. Absentminded even then. He'd forget what assignment he'd given us and we'd stall around, ask him questions, and he'd end by talking about some pet idea all through the period. We used to get away with murder."

"It looks," Jake said, "like someone won't get away with murder. Hall Masson has come back to run down his brother's killer. Just came over the radio."

Harry gave his twisted smile. "I've heard about Hall. He's another historian like old Burgess. He won't trouble us long."

VII

To reach the bleak little room in the basement where Frank Burgess, as a volunteer, worked to salvage some of the dropouts of Shelton, boys who had been in marginal trouble with the law, and those who were beginning to turn into young punks, Jake had to go through the library and down a circular iron staircase.

Even on a swelteringly hot afternoon like this one the library was cool and so was Miss Carlyle, the librarian. She was tall for a girl, as tall as Jake, and she made herself even taller by high heels and her superb carriage. Jake could never make up his mind whether she was pretty or not. Her hair and eyes were brown and so, in mid-July, was her skin. When she was excited or interested her face lighted up in what was real beauty. When she was tired or bored she appeared almost plain. More than anything it was her voice that attracted Jake, a low-pitched voice, sexy he thought. She spoke so slowly that her words seemed to be spaced but you could tell by her eyes that she thought quickly.

Jake, whose normal attitude was one of insolence and defiance, was meek with Miss Carlyle. He wouldn't admit to himself that he was
afraid of her brother Gregory but he had a
healthy respect for that young man's temper.
He had once seen him go into action, smashing
a guy so hard that he'd been had up for assault.

Today Miss Carlyle sat at her desk doodling
on a pad. She did not even turn her head when
some girls began giggling back in the stacks,
though as a rule she stopped a disturbance
at once.

"Afternoon, Miss Carlyle."

"Go right down, Jake. Mr. Burgess is waiting for you."

This, it appeared, was one of her dull days.
Usually she asked him how he was getting
on.

He clattered down the iron staircase to the
room where old Burgess was waiting. Around
the walls were stacks holding books that were
rarely called for, newspapers and magazines.
At a bare table in the middle of the room old
Burgess was trying to read under an unshaded
droplight. His knuckles were swollen by ar-
thritis, his nose seemed to grow bigger as his
face became more shrunken. For a moment
he looked up over his glasses as though he
did not recognize Jake. Then he nodded to
the chair across from him.

The interview progressed as it always did. Jake didn't see any of his old gang, he said virtuously. He was working steady at Harry's garage and taking home his earnings except for five dollars a week. He was, he lied blandly, doing homework to make up his grades. He was, he added truthfully, taking swimming and diving lessons twice a week at the Halsted pool. The gymnasium for the town boys that Mr. Halsted had built would be open in another week. He had already signed up.

"So you are finding the summer interesting, after all," Burgess said in his gentle voice.

"It's going to be interesting all right." Jake smiled maliciously. "Hall Masson is back, the lieutenant's brother. He says he's come to find his brother's killer. That ought to warm things up."

Burgess sat quite still, his bluish lips gathering in, blowing out. "No," he said at last. "Oh, no! He must be stopped. One way or another he must be stopped." Abruptly he pushed back his chair, reached for an ancient floppy straw hat and went up the stairs.

Jake stared after him and then shrugged. The afternoon's session was apparently over. By the time he got upstairs the old man had already left the library.

Miss Carlyle seemed to have snapped out of her daydream or whatever had engrossed her. "Anything wrong? Mr. Burgess looked ill. I hope the heat isn't affecting him."

Jake grinned. "The old man thinks he can stop Lieutenant Masson's brother from gunning down the killer." He shook his long hair out of his eyes. "Looks to me, Miss Carlyle, like Shelton is going to have a real hot summer."

TWO

There was no train service to Shelton but a bus from the Port Authority Terminal in New York City made the trip four times a day. Even after weeks in Egypt the heat in New York struck Hall Masson like a blast from a furnace. A thermometer at the airport read 97.

"Going up to 103 today," the taxi driver said with gloomy satisfaction. "Weeks of it. Weeks and weeks. And no rain. Well, like they say, people talk about the weather but they don't do anything about it."

As usual New York seemed fantastically beautiful to the returned traveler. Blindingly beautiful. Literally. The relentless sun reflected on steel and glass, dazzling the eyes, as Hall clipped dark plastic lenses over his horn-rimmed spectacles.

As the taxi inched its way across Forty-second Street fumes from exhaust in the bumper-to-bumper traffic added to the intolerable discomfort. Already the treacherous humidity was making Hall perspire. He took off his hat and wiped his face. Along the sidewalk people moved like a slow-motion movie, struggling for position in the narrow patch of shade beside the buildings, the men coatless, the women wearing as little as the law permitted, with a few borderline cases.

A bus for Shelton was scheduled to leave in ten minutes and it was, fortunately, air-conditioned. Before taking a seat Hall looked at the other passengers but there was no one he recognized. He would be home in less than two hours. Home? Hardly. In the past five years he had rarely visited the place. The aunt who had brought up Hall and Robin had stated her position clearly.

"I've done all I can for you, Hall. You know that. Treated you both alike. That's true, whatever you may say."

"I haven't said anything." He was smiling.

"If I've loved Robin more — well, you can't love to order."

"Of course not." He grinned at her distress. "Matter of fact, I like Robin better myself."

"The thing is," she had said that afternoon more than five years ago, "I've done my best. I've brought you up and educated you. I planned to help establish each of you in the field in which you wanted to work. But this — you say fifteen thousand is absolutely essential. Then I'm afraid it is the last I can do for you. Otherwise I wouldn't be fair to Robin. If you are positive you want this money now, you've got to be on your own in the future. You understand that?"

"I understand." Hall looked at the troubled face and bent impulsively to kiss her cheek. "It's all right," he assured her.

That evening he packed his clothes and books — except for books he had never accumulated possessions; Robin said that he gathered no moss — and the next day he arranged for a tutoring job. In spite of his aunt's claim that she had provided his education he had won top scholarships year after year. But he still had to obtain his doctorate before he could teach.

Actually he had never taught. He could not afford to wait for the doctorate. After doing hack jobs of research and rewriting, he began to lecture and write on contemporary history. He had never seen his aunt after that interview, but nothing had altered his relationship with his younger brother. Perhaps their very differences had made them so close, so companionable. Robin had been the one who made life exciting; he was a creature of action rather than thought. Hall had been more at home in the world of ideas. Always it was Robin who provided the leadership and Hall the balance.

Robin had laughed when Hall decided that he wanted to teach history.

"I," he said, "prefer to make history."

And so, in the brief span allotted him, he did. A hero at twenty-five. But a dead hero. Bitter grief engulfed Hall. And hatred. He would track down the killer who had shot Robin and his pretty little Lillian if it took the rest of his life.

The bus stop was only a block from the lower end of the Village Green. For a moment Hall stood, suitcase, typewriter, and briefcase at his feet, looking around him. There was a new supermarket in what had been fields beyond the town, its parking lot half filled. For some reason he felt outraged. He had experienced this same senseless reaction before, had been disturbed to find that no one can return to the place he has left, only to the place it has become. Some subconscious and idiotic ego, he supposed, made one imagine that nothing happened except in the place where one was.

The air was hot here, too, but not like New York. There were no subways or steel buildings to hold the heat. Shelton was a village of trees.

Hall turned as a car horn blared impatiently and moved aside so it could draw up at the gas pumps of Harry's Service Station. That was new, too. Sparkling new. On this corner, Hall recalled, a house had stood since the late seventeen hundreds. The Shelton Historical

Society had maintained it and held meetings there.

Progress, he told himself. What are you looking for, the good old days? Any historian knows there weren't any. All that counts is learning by our mistakes and building better for the future, which sounded fine if he could only think of a nation or a man capable of learning by experience.

A boy who had been putting gas in the car turned to stare at Hall. Seventeen, perhaps, long fair hair that hung over his neck and over his forehead into his eyes. At first glance he resembled a girl, at second glance a sheep dog. A sullen mouth with no promise of strength, eyes that were already furtive. A young punk, Hall thought dispassionately. The boy ran back to the office to make change. When he returned he was followed by a heavy-set man with a scarred face on which a grafting job had been done. Younger than I am, Hall thought, but the kind who never looked young. The man stood examining Hall, the fingers of one hand concealing his mouth. Then he approached, thrust out a thick hand.

"Welcome home, Mr. Masson."

"You know me?" Hall said in surprise. "I'm afraid —"

"You look like your brother. A hell of a

29

lot like your brother." Harry laughed. "Going to give people quite a shock. Of course you wear glasses and you're older and," after an insolent scrutiny the garage man added, "tougher. And naturally we knew you were coming. That interview you gave the press this morning. And that reminds me, a reporter stopped by just a few minutes ago. New York paper. Wanted a story about you."

"There won't be a story until I've accomplished what I came here to do."

Harry fingered his lips. "I had you sized up wrong. Absent-minded professor type like old Burgess. I thought this was going to be strictly for laughs. Let it go, Masson. Get lost." As Hall watched him he added, "That way no one gets hurt."

To Jake, a fascinated spectator in the office doorway, it seemed that neither man intended to move. Then the one who looked so disturbingly like Lieutenant Masson said, "I may be around here quite a while. Do you have a second-hand car in good condition that I can rent or buy?"

"Bring around that Buick convertible, Jake." Harry turned to Hall. "Last year's model and the owner was an invalid who rarely used it. Just the one driver. Not four thousand miles on it."

Hall nodded gravely. "Astonishing how

often that happens." He grinned at Harry. "Let's give it a trial run."

II

Somewhat to his surprise, for he wouldn't have trusted Harry an inch, Hall found that the Buick ran like a charm. The price was exorbitant but he was in a hurry and in no mood to haggle.

Behind the wheel of the Buick he drove along the Green, eyes straight ahead though he could not miss seeing the white obelisk which dominated the village. When he visited the Hero's Corner he wanted to be without witnesses and now there were people sitting in the shade under the trees on the Green.

The Cape Cod house looked smaller than he had remembered it, while the hedges and bushes were much larger. All the windows were wide open so someone must be there. He hadn't been sure and he wouldn't ask Harry, who probably knew. He had relied on his own key, but he was relieved to know that it wouldn't be necessary.

For a moment after he stopped the car his heart sank. Suppose someone else had bought the house and moved in. Then he remembered Robin's long-distance telephone call the day he was married. His voice had

31

been gay and exultant.

"I've made a will and left you the works, the house and the money, in case anything should happen to me."

"You're married now," Hall had reminded him.

"Lillian will get her uncle's estate and that's ten times what I have. Anyhow —"

Hall had checked him quickly. "Anyhow, I am seven years older."

"But so damned careful, Hall. You'll live to be a dull old man." Robin had given his disarming laugh. "You probably won't get much. I'm not the kind to save for my old age."

A woman came out on the front step of the Cape Cod and put up a hand to shield her eyes as she peered through the brilliant sunlight to where the Buick was parked in the shade.

"No canvassers," she called, and added as an afterthought, "and no reporters."

Hall got out of the car and came toward her. "Mrs. Cushing?"

Her hand crept to her corded throat as she stared at him. The housekeeper had not changed at all in the years since he had seen her. This was one thing that had remained the same.

"It's Mr. Masson! Good lord, you gave me

32

a turn. I'd forgotten how much you look like Mr. Robert." She shook hands with him, studying him frankly. "Don't know why I was so taken aback, because I was expecting you. Heard that interview you gave at the airport so I did some quick shopping for your dinner and made up a bed. Same room you used to have. It's hot up there under the eaves but I knew you wouldn't be staying."

She led the way into the house, which at first seemed unfamiliar. His aunt's clutter of possessions had been removed except for a few fine pieces of furniture. The house was light and gay and more spacious.

"It's different," he said, looking around.

"Young Mrs. Masson loved fixing the place up. After that big house of the Halsteds this was like a doll's house to her. She was always the brightest, happiest thing." And unexpectedly the housekeeper was crying.

Hall eased her into a chair, went to the kitchen for a glass of water. The kitchen, too, was gay and colorful. When he had put the glass in Mrs. Cushing's hand and she had sipped it, the sobbing stopped.

"I found her," she said at last. "I found them both. I'll never forget it. They were so young and so beautiful to look at."

"Tell me about it." Hall's voice was quiet as he drew up a chair facing her.

Mrs. Cushing got up hastily. "Letting myself go like that! And you just home. I'm ashamed. I'll bring you some iced tea. No trouble because it's already made and there's some fresh mint from the garden."

Hall listened to her footsteps as she hurried out to the kitchen. She had stopped just short of breaking into a run. Although she had said that the tea was already made, it was nearly a quarter of an hour before she returned, carrying a tall glass of iced tea, with a sprig of fresh mint and a sliver of lemon on the plate with its folded linen napkin.

"I was thinking," she began briskly, "that it's just as well you stopped by Shelton for a few days. You can go over the house and select anything you want to keep. I suppose you could get a better price for the place furnished." Her eyes avoided his, her hands pleated the skirt of her dress.

He sipped the tea, which was strong and chilled. There was a breeze through the living room and the almost forgotten scent of potpourri from two ancient Chinese bowls on the mantel.

"We'd better get things clear, Mrs. Cushing. I am not passing through Shelton. I intend to stay here until I clear up the story of my brother's murder. Two charming and harmless young people were shot down in cold blood and no one seems to have a clue. More than that, I begin to think that no one wants to know who killed them. You're the second person to try to warn me off since I reached the village. I'm staying." He finished the tea and lighted his pipe, prepared to wait indefinitely.

At length, as though they had fought a silent battle of wills, she heaved a long sigh, acknowledging defeat. "What do you want me to tell you?"

"Who killed them?"

"But I haven't the faintest idea!" she exclaimed, and he heard the ring of truth in her voice.

"Tell me what happened, as far as you know it."

Mrs. Cushing was not a good reporter. Her thinking was disorganized, she rambled, and she could not distinguish the relevant from the irrelevant. While she had already told this story many times — to the doctor, the police, Lillian's overwrought uncle and aunt, the neighbors, her friends — it was far from coherent.

"I came that morning at eight o'clock, my regular time, because the young people slept late as a rule and didn't want breakfast much before nine-thirty. I washed last night's dishes — Mrs. Masson liked to get dinner herself, you never saw so many cookbooks in your life — and then she stacked the dishes in the sink.

"They must have had company the night before because there were extra dishes and glasses and they had finished the bottle of gin. Half full it had been when I left.

"Well, I did the dishes and cleaned up the kitchen real good and took the soiled tablecloth and napkins down to the basement and stuck them in the electric washer with some dishtowels and stuff I'd been saving up for a full load.

"When I came back I went to the dining room to set the table for breakfast. I always worked real quiet because Mr. Robert," her voice thickened, "you know how he was. Always joking. He said he didn't mind my hurling the crockery about but he didn't see why I liked to throw it through the windowpane. Just his way of talking, you know.

"Well, as I say, they usually slept late but you could hear them when they woke up, talking and laughing, or the shower going, or — sometimes they didn't come down for quite a while.

"It was getting on for nine-thirty when I finished setting the table. There wasn't a sound from upstairs and I thought it must have been a very late party."

"Who had been the guests? Do you know?"

Mrs. Cushing shook her head. "I didn't even know they were planning to entertain. Usually Mrs. Masson would tell me and have me get out extra dishes or buy something special or send me to that new shop for some kind of herb. She was a great one for using herbs."

Hall realized that the housekeeper was deliberately postponing the hard part of her story.

"Anyhow, I put some coffee on — sometimes they liked a cup of coffee before they had breakfast. I was going out to get the cream — the milkman won't deliver beyond the driveway and this time of year if you don't get it right in the refrigerator it turns sour — so I walked in here and then I saw Mrs. Masson. She was lying over there on the couch and first I thought she was asleep, and then I saw the stain on her pretty dinner dress and it was blood.

"For a moment I couldn't even move and then I screamed for Mr. Robert and began to run toward the couch though I knew — she was so still — and then I saw him. He was lying on the floor and there was a hole in his forehead and his eyes and mouth were wide open."

She waited to steady her voice. "Somehow I got to the phone and called Mr. Halsted because he was her uncle and right next door. And then I must have passed out. When I came to, I was in the bedroom Mr. Robert had before he was married and it seemed like everyone was here: the Halsteds, the doctor, the police, people all over the place."

When Hall said nothing she went on, "I answered about a million questions and then I started laughing and crying and the doctor gave me something."

The telephone rang and she went out to the small phone booth off the foyer to answer it.

"For you," she said, coming back to the door.

He looked at her in some surprise. "Who knows I am here?"

Her expression was curious. "Everyone, so far as I can make out. Half the village has called already and a New York reporter came just before you did. I got rid of him in short order, I can tell you. It's Mr. Halsted now."

As Hall went past her she said, "Go easy with him, Mr. Masson. Mrs. Masson's death just about killed him. He hasn't been the same since."

THREE

"A drink?" Bruce Halsted asked.

When Hall had last seen him he had resembled Mark Twain, particularly when he wore the white suits to which he was addicted in summer. Now he appeared to have aged twenty years in the five that had passed since their last meeting. The resonance was gone from his voice, the firmness from his handshake. Oddly enough, his mouselike wife seemed to have taken on added character and decision.

"It's rather hot for a cocktail," Hall demurred.

"Gin and tonic?"

"That would be fine."

When the glasses had been passed — Mrs. Halsted had asked for tonic without the gin — there was a moment's awkward pause. Halsted lifted his glass, set it down again.

"I can't seem to think of a suitable toast," he admitted.

Hall raised his own glass. "To the truth."

"No," Mrs. Halsted protested. "No, Hall, you simply must not do it. Let things alone."

"Let someone get away with two murders?"

39

"Bruce," Mrs. Halsted said in appeal, "you tell him."

"Harriet is right, Hall. All you can do is harm."

Hall looked in perplexity from one to the other. The old man was haggard, his wife's usual negation turned to a tigerlike quality, a chick prepared to defend a fighting cock. It was laughable, it was perplexing, it was disturbing.

"I intend to find my brother's murderer. Nothing under God's heaven is going to stop me. Is that clear? I can't understand either of you. Lillian was like your own child."

"Let her rest," Halsted said. "Let them both rest."

"As a simple matter of justice —"

"Justice is never a simple matter," Halsted said unexpectedly. "Like truth, no two people could define it in the same way, certainly no two people. It's relative. It's —"

"Are you trying to say that, in this case, it's unobtainable?"

"You aren't looking for justice," Mrs. Halsted told him, "you're looking for vengeance, like the Furies. There's something — wait." She searched for the book on the table, turned pages. "Here it is about the Furies: 'Their office was to pursue and punish sinners. They were called those who walk in darkness.' Vengeance isn't justice. It isn't civilized. The Greeks were always seeking vengeance. Like one of those feuds in primitive parts of the South. They just go on and on. All that happens is that more and more people get hurt. Let it alone, Hall."

There was a long pause. Hall sat shaking the chilled glass idly, hearing the ice tinkle. "Everyone wants to stop me. Why?"

The Halsteds exchanged glances and then the old man made a pleading gesture. It was his wife who explained. "We loved Robin and he was a hero not only to this village but to young people everywhere. You loved him, too, Hall. Don't take that away from him. We've been shielding him the best we could."

"What does that mean?"

Halsted said wearily, "There was no intruder that night. Not a trace of one. Lillian and Robin were both shot with his own revolver."

"I don't believe it."

"It was lying beside his hand. I was the first one there except for Mrs. Cushing who was too upset to notice anything. I took it away. That seemed the only way to protect Robin's memory."

"It hadn't occurred to you that the truth might clear him?"

"The facts spoke for themselves. I buried

the revolver in the rose bed."

After a long time Hall asked, "Why would Robin shoot his wife and then commit suicide? Why, for God's sake?"

"I don't know."

"Have you told the police this interesting theory of yours?"

Halsted flinched at the younger man's savage tone. If only Hall didn't look so disturbingly like his brother! Of course he was older, less good-looking. He had none of Robin's boyish charm. The horn-rimmed glasses made a difference, too. His voice was deeper, more resonant. He didn't smile as easily as Robin. He was, Halsted thought, altogether a harder man.

"Of course he didn't tell them! That's what he is trying to explain," Harriet said impatiently. "Bruce has suffered enough. I won't have you talking to him like that."

Like a wren attacking a hawk to save its nest, Hall reflected, watching Harriet's anxious eyes as they rested on her husband's ravaged face, wondering what she was really afraid of. He had always been fond of the Halsteds, who had in many ways sweetened the lives of the two brothers; who had known that a little indulgence is as necessary as discipline to small boys. But his affection would not deter him from wringing the truth out of them

42

in one way or another.

"Mrs. Halsted, do you really expect me to believe that you lived next door to them for four months, that you saw them daily, and you didn't know anything was wrong, so wrong it could lead to murder and suicide? Not for a single moment? You never saw Robin do anything queer? You never saw Lillian afraid of him, unhappy with him?"

"She was so in love she'd never have told me if she was afraid or unhappy. She'd have protected him if she could."

Halsted slammed down his drink, snapping the fragile glass. "For God's sake, let it alone!"

"If I keep on looking, what do you think I'll find?" Hall asked.

"That obelisk down there meant a lot to Robin. Few men ever saw a memorial erected to them during their lifetime. I believe he'd have died willingly to keep it — unstained."

"And that's why he shot himself?"

"That's why."

Hall stood up, looked from one tense face to the other.

"I don't believe it."

II

At eleven that night the Green was deserted. There was no sound except for the passing

of an occasional car. Hall had come at last
to the Hero's Corner with its white stone obelisk, a metal plaque at the base reading: "This
stone has been erected to express the eternal
gratitude of Shelton to its most magnificent
citizen, Lieutenant Robert Masson." Beneath
it there were several wreaths, some fresh flowers, and some tuberous begonias in pots.

Hall's brief visit to the cemetery with its
two new graves had not brought him closer
to Robin. But here, with the love and admiration of his brother's friends and neighbors
made manifest, he leaned back on the Green
bench and let his mind wander, to seek and
find his brother's bright spirit as it would.
For the first time the bitter grief of his loss
was lessened, became bearable. After a long
while he lighted his pipe but still he did not
move.

A kind of wordless communication seemed
to be established with Robin, who was, he
thought, glad that he had returned. Robin had
always come to him with his perplexities and
problems, though, God knows, there had been
few of those. He had given his older brother
deep affection and absolute trust. Even when
he rejected Hall's advice he admitted, laughing, that he was probably right.

"Solemn old codger! You know what you'll
end up by being like? Old Burgess, the guy

who knows all the right answers."

"There is no such animal. And you'll end up in the soup. Those girls of yours! How many do you have on the string now? Who's the latest? Jenny?"

"Oh, that's off," Robin said. "I saw her with Bill Galling at the club dance. When I can't have them to myself I don't want them at all."

Hall laughed. "And you dating three at a time! You can't have it both ways."

"I can try." Robin had grinned at him.

Hall stirred restlessly. He hadn't come here for trivial memories like that. The trouble was that memory played queer tricks. It wasn't the big things you remembered. They slipped away somewhere into the dim recesses of the mind. It was the little things that remained fresh and bright.

The sound of shots from a television set that had been tuned too high in one of the gracious white houses on the Green roused him from his musing. He tried to assess the day that had passed. He had set out to discover Robin's killer and from the moment when he stepped off the bus in Shelton he had encountered nothing but obstruction. Harry the garage man had warned him off. Mrs. Cushing had suggested hopefully that he was stopping only for a few days. The Halsteds had tried to make him believe that Robin had shot his wife and then had committed suicide.

"I don't believe it," Hall said aloud, and beside hin someone gasped.

He turned to see the girl who had seated herself quietly on the bench beside him, a tall girl, hatless, dark hair lifted softly by the breeze. Her eyes were wide and startled. He looked down and noticed that she had very pretty legs. He noticed also that she had chosen the only occupied bench on the Green.

"Sorry I startled you. I have a bad habit of talking to myself." He spoke courteously but he wished she would go away. He wanted to be alone.

"Perhaps," she said, speaking slowly, "that's because you don't talk enough to other people."

He looked at her in surprise, trying to make out her expression. "You couldn't be more mistaken. I spend a good third of my life on the lecture platform."

"That's not talking to people; that's talking at them."

He laughed shortly. "You may be right."

"The trouble with doing all the talking," the persistent girl went on, "is that you not only supply the questions; you have to supply the answers, too."

He was amused. When she fumbled in her handbag for a cigarette he leaned forward to light it for her, taking advantage of the opportunity to get a good look at her face. She was, he discovered, exceptionally pretty, probably high intelligence, a look of breeding. This obviously wasn't a pickup, but why had she chosen the one bench that was occupied?

"What's wrong," he asked when he had snapped off his lighter, "with supplying the answers?"

"You have to be awfully sure you are right." When he made no reply she asked, "What do you base your answers on, Mr. Masson?" As he looked at her in surprise she said, "You look like your brother. Incredibly like him. And you were here, worshiping at the shrine."

Hall had never before wanted to strike a woman. It was a new experience and an unpleasant one. After a pause he asked, "Did you know Robin?"

"I met him several times." She did not seem inclined to add to her statement.

"And his wife?"

"I — suppose I've seen her around the village."

"You must have moved here after I left."

"After your aunt asked you to leave. At least that's the way I heard it."

Hall knocked out his pipe. "When I give

answers I rely on evidence and not on hearsay. Tell me, what do you really dislike me for?"

"Because you've come here like an avenging fury to destroy everything in your path as long as you can find out who fired the shots at Lillian and Robert Masson."

"An avenging fury. That's the second time today someone has called me that."

"Don't you mind?"

"At the moment, Miss — uh —"

"I am Gail Carlyle." She flung the name at him like a challenge.

"At the moment, I am not particularly interested in my public image, Miss Carlyle. I do care about Robin's."

"No one will smear his image if you don't interfere. Why can't you let well enough alone? Go away, Mr. Masson. Stick to your own profession. Forget all this."

"You are very fervent, very dramatic. Perhaps you should be the lecturer."

His mockery stung her. She dropped her cigarette and stepped on it. As she stood up he got to his feet.

"Mr. Masson, for the last time, will you abandon this stupid plan of yours and go away?"

"I'll go away when I've done what I came here to do. Not before."

"What you will do will be to tear down that

obelisk and hurt innocent people, perhaps destroy them."

"I'm getting rather tired of repeating this, Miss Carlyle, but someone shot my brother to death. Someone killed his wife. I intend to know why. I intend to know who."

Her eyes were only a few inches below his own. "How do you expect to do that?"

"I'm going to find out who wanted them to be dead. That's what it really adds up to, isn't it?"

"You won't like what you find."

The girl turned and walked away across the Green. With part of his mind he observed that she walked beautifully. He heard her heels tapping down the street and looked after her until she had passed the ivy-covered library and turned the corner. Her smoldering mood, a combination of hostility with a kind of fear, had robbed the Green of its peace. He could no longer feel Robin's presence. He took the steep road above the Green.

III

As he walked up the gravel driveway to the Cape Cod cottage he heard the rusty creaking of the lawn swing and stopped short.

"That you, Hall?" The motion of the swing halted. "I've been waiting for you."

Hall recognized the gentle voice. "Mr. Burgess!"

"Imagine you remembering the old man!" The former teacher sounded pleased.

"How could I forget you? You sparked my interest in history, you know."

"I heard you were back and dropped by for a chat. But if it's a bad time —" The old man paused uncertainly. "I'm forgetful. You've had a long trip and a sad one. I don't sleep much any more so I prowl at all hours. I don't always remember that young people need their rest."

"Come in and have a nightcap," Hall suggested.

"It's cooler out here and I don't drink much these days."

"Then I'll get a can of beer for myself and join you." When Hall came back he switched on the outside light and the old teacher looked up, startled.

"You'll attract bugs," he protested.

Hall turned out the light. If the old man preferred sitting in the dark that was all right with him. Anyhow there had been time to see what he was beginning to look for. Like everyone he had spoken to in Shelton the old man was afraid. Hall settled in a deep canvas chair on the lawn and tilted back the frosty beer can.

After a while Burgess said gently, "I'm sorry it happened, Hall."

"So am I."

"There's not much else to say, is there?"

"Except — why."

"You won't just leave it alone?"

"No."

The old man sighed. "You always had the tenacity of a bulldog."

"I'm going to need it this time. There's a general conspiracy to drive me out of town, to make me drop this search of mine. Even the Halsteds. Good God, even the Halsteds! And yet they adored Lillian."

"Did you know your sister-in-law well?"

"Just casually. She ran with a much younger crowd when she was here and most of the time she was in a boarding school in Switzerland. When she came back to stay I was away lecturing, and I haven't been back. Of course I've always known the Halsteds."

"They spoiled her," Burgess said reflectively. "Natural enough in the circumstances. They let her have her own way. Even about marrying Robert."

"Why shouldn't she?"

"Well, for one thing he was older."

"Only seven years. That's not such a hell of a difference."

"But seventy years in experience. She

couldn't expect to be able to bridge that. War changes people. Bound to. You didn't see Robin after he was discharged from the army, did you?"

"No, I was on a lecture tour in Australia and then a magazine sent me to Egypt to gather material for some articles, eventually, I hope, a book."

"And you haven't been back here in recent years." When Hall made no comment Burgess asked, "Why?"

"My aunt more or less kicked me out. And what," Hall demanded, "has that to do with Lillian's death?"

"It just might," the old man answered as he hauled himself out of the lawn swing, "be the answer to it."

"What are you trying to tell me?" In spite of himself Hall's voice was strained.

"All I can tell you is that the day before her death Lillian was frightened out of her wits. She came to the library — I have an office in the basement — crying and carrying on. Miss Carlyle, the librarian, had to be pretty sharp with her for making a disturbance."

FOUR

As Mrs. Cushing had pointed out, it was hot in the small attic room that Hall had occupied as a boy. Even with the door and window wide open there was no breeze. At length he ripped the sheets off the bed and went downstairs to the larger room that had been Robin's until his marriage.

Hall pulled off the cover and made up the bed. There was cross-ventilation here and the room was much more comfortable. Robin had always been given the best things, a situation which Hall had accepted as matter-of-factly as Robin himself, and without resentment. There was a kind of shining quality about Robin. He had much the same impact on people that Rupert Brooke was said to have made, though he wasn't, of course, so startlingly handsome.

Before turning out the light Hall looked around the room in which Robin had lived until he went off to war. It was still a boy's room. The pictures on the wall were of various athletic groups with Robin's laughing face easily distinguishable. The blank places, Hall surmised, had held pictures of girls tactfully removed when Robin married Lillian. Girls had always flung themselves at Robin's head but, though he had not been a young man to pass up an opportunity, he had rarely been the pursuer. Only when he met Lillian did he really fall in love. Now the Halsteds suggested that Lillian had died at Robin's hand. And the Halsteds were frightened.

Though he had had little sleep Hall was too restless to go to bed. He paced the floor, pausing to look down at the Green where the white pillar of the obelisk soared proudly. How had this constant reminder of his neighbors' esteem affected Robin? It was a lot to live up to.

Looking back now, Hall found it difficult to remember what his reaction had been when he had learned, only forty-eight hours earlier, of Robin's death. After the first shock and grief and bitter sense of loss he had assumed that the two deaths had been caused by a housebreaker caught in the act or a mental case who had gone berserk. Anything but what he had found, that the village had established a conspiracy of silence, that the village was afraid. More monstrous, that Bruce Halsted believed that Robin and Lillian had been shot by Robin's own hand.

Frowning, he went over that curious conversation with the Carlyle girl. *You won't like what you find. Destroy innocent people, smear the obelisk.* What the hell had been going on in Shelton? What were people, even old Burgess, afraid that he would uncover?

Worshiping at the shrine. The girl had hated Robin.

That was for sure. But what could Robin possibly have done to her, unless she had been one of the girls who had fallen in love with him? Hell hath no fury.

"I'll shake the truth out of someone," Hall promised himself savagely. "I'll tear this village apart until I get at the truth."

Tired of pacing the floor he examined Robin's bookshelf in search of something to read. A boy's collection: adventure stories, science fiction, a few textbooks, a library book that should have been returned months before. Tomorrow, Hall decided, he would return the book and have a talk with Miss Carlyle, who claimed not to know Lillian but who had been overheard having a quarrel with her.

On the verge of falling asleep, Hall remembered Burgess's curious suggestion that there might be a connection between Lillian's death and the fact that his aunt had disinherited him and kicked him out. He followed the reflection of a car's lights as they moved ghostlike across the ceiling. No, he decided, it can't be that. Only one person ever knew.

In the morning he would visit the State Police and find out what their investigation had unearthed. If anything.

He was having a spirited encounter with a trooper when the clank of milk bottles awakened him. Yawning he got out of bed and went to take a shower. The smell of frying bacon greeted him as he came downstairs.

"Would you like a cup of coffee now?" Mrs. Cushing asked. "Your breakfast will be ready in a few minutes. I started it as soon as I heard the shower running." When she had brought him the coffee she said, "It's going to be another scorcher. Last night didn't cool off as much as usual. That room of yours must have been a hot box."

"It was. I moved into my brother's old room. I'll be here indefinitely, Mrs. Cushing. I'd like to have you stay on, if you will, and get my dinners, too. As I recall, Shelton doesn't have any restaurants."

There was a long pause and then Mrs. Cushing said, "If that's the way you want it, Mr. Masson." Her manner was stiff with disapproval.

He smiled at her. "Good coffee, Mrs. Cushing." He added smoothly, "Why don't you want me to stay?" He brushed aside her flustered denials, waited for an answer. Once more she capitulated.

"I just don't know and that's a fact, Mr. Masson. Only I can't help feeling things are best left alone."

"Why?"

"There was something wrong," she said reluctantly. "The first month they were married was all honeymoon. But after that — not that he wasn't crazy about her, I don't mean that; only something bothered Mr. Robert."

"Bothered?"

Her hands twisted in frustration over the inadequate word. "Well, he changed somehow. Like he was worried. And he'd sort of watch Mrs. Masson in an anxious sort of way. Oh, dear, I don't know how to express it. And he'd stand looking out at that obelisk with the strangest — and once he said," she went on incoherently, "when Mrs. Masson was admiring it, that it was a load to carry. Only George Washington, he said, could have managed to hold up a weight like that."

"Nothing specific, then?"

"Just," Mrs. Cushing said, "that it's better not to stir things up. Oh, I forgot to tell you, there's a letter on the hall table. I found it on the floor this morning."

A letter drop in the front door spilled mail onto the carpet inside. The letter had no postmark, it was typewritten and unsigned: "Get out of town before you get hurt."

57

When he had read it for the third time, Hall folded it carefully and put it in his pocket. He was smiling when he sat down to breakfast.

Mrs. Cushing was surprised and pleased by his healthy appetite. "Good news?"

"The best," he assured her. "Someone is beginning to panic."

II

He was still smiling when he went out to get in the Buick. Then the smile faded. All four tires had been slashed. For a long time he stood staring at the wanton damage. Someone wanted action, did he? Well, by God, he was going to get it. He went back to the house to call Harry's Service Station.

"This is Hall Masson. Someone having fun and games slashed all the tires on my car."

"Now that's too bad."

"How soon can you fix it up?"

"Well, we're pretty busy today."

"I said — how soon?"

"Maybe I can get someone out there this afternoon. Maybe not until tomorrow." He wasn't trying to be cooperative or to conceal his amusement over the situation.

"You're beginning to interest me, Harry," Hall said softly and broke the connection. Then he called the State Police. This time he couldn't complain of a lack of interest.

"You say you are Hall Masson?"

"That's right."

"Stay there, will you? We'll have a man out in ten minutes."

They did better than that. The car with the state insignia pulled up behind the Buick in exactly six minutes. The young man in a trim uniform, who said he was Trooper Purdy, stood surveying the damaged Buick. The older man in plain clothes, who introduced himself as Captain Gerfind, walked toward the front door where Hall was waiting for him.

"The living room is on the right," Hall said, standing back for the captain to precede him.

"Yes, I know. I've been here before."

"Investigating the murders?"

"Yes." The captain looked at him briefly, looked away. The guy was taking it hard, but who could blame him? "I heard you were back. You gave an interview."

"That bunch of ghouls was waiting at the airport. They took me by surprise." Hall added, "I hope I wasn't stepping on your toes. I realize you are competent to handle the investigation without my help."

The captain looked around the room, remembering what it had been like on the morning when he had come in answer to Halsted's horrified call.

59

"You look like the lieutenant," he said at last. "I guess you know that Shelton people thought a lot of him."

"So did I. Too much to let his murder go by default."

The captain wasn't offended but he wasn't apologetic either. He gave the impression of a man who was comfortably on the top of his job but not complacent. An honest cop, Hall thought, and an efficient one.

"We've been investigating, Mr. Masson. We are doing everything we can."

"But you've found no trace, no clue to the person who shot my brother and his wife. No motive. Nothing."

"It isn't quite that bad. And we haven't quit. We won't quit. I want you to understand that. It's not merely that your brother was the town's hero, or that his wife was a young and lovely girl, or even that her uncle has done more for this place than anyone else in its history. We don't like murder here."

"Have you found anything at all?"

"We've dug up some curious facts but we haven't been able to fit them into a picture yet. Of course, there's always the possibility that the murderer cleared out of town after he had killed them. He might be in Alaska now, so far as we know."

"Whoever did it is still around."

"How do you figure that?"

"The tires, for one thing. This letter, for another." Hall handed it over. "More than anything else, a concerted effort on the part of everyone I've met to drive me away."

Captain Gerfind read the letter and, after a questioning look, pocketed it. "You sure about that?"

"I don't suffer from a persecution complex," Hall said dryly, "and I have been trained to check and recheck information before accepting it as reliable."

Gerfind went to the door and signaled the trooper, who came in, looked once at the couch, and then moved to the window seat, opening his notebook.

"Now," the captain said, "suppose you tell me about it."

Hall described his conversation with Harry who had told him to get lost, that way no one would get hurt; with Mrs. Cushing, who expected him to leave; with the Halsteds, who begged him to give up his search; with Gail Carlyle; with Frank Burgess. All that he left out was Halsted's claim that Robin and Lillian had been killed with Robin's own revolver. He explained to himself that he did not want to get Halsted in trouble for concealing evidence.

"On top of that, there's the anonymous letter; I found all four tires slashed this morning, and Harry doesn't seem to be in a hurry to repair them. Add it up and something stinks to high heaven. I can tell you this: the whole damned village can't drive me away."

When the captain made no comment Hall added, "It's your turn."

"We answered Mr. Halsted's call about nine-fifty in the morning. He had been informed by the housekeeper, who discovered the bodies. You know, I suppose, what we found. Mrs. Masson was lying on the couch with a bullet through her heart. Mr. Masson was on the carpet near the door, a bullet through his forehead. He, too, was fully dressed. There was no sign of the weapon.

"No one heard the shots. The nearest house is the Halsteds' which is fully air-conditioned. The next one is the Williamses', newcomers here, who heard nothing.

"Dr. Morgan, who did the post-mortems, came up with a queer thing. He said, judging by the stomach contents, that Mrs. Masson had been dead for about ten hours and Mr. Masson for not more than seven. We've been stumbling over that one ever since. Another thing. No one has come forward and admitted seeing the Massons that night, though Mrs. Cushing was sure they had at least two guests for dinner, judging by the number of extra dirty dishes and glasses. Unfortunately she had cleared everything up before she discovered the crimes. We've combed the names of every friend the Massons were supposed to know and drawn a blank."

"What about enemies?" Hall asked. "Somewhere in this village is someone who hated Robin's guts. I want to know why."

"Leave this to us, Mr. Masson. You'll only be getting in the way and stepping on a lot of toes."

"I'll be kicking in a lot of teeth, if necessary. Don't make any mistake about that. Do you help or do you hinder?"

Gerfind grinned. "We're not allowed to kick people in the teeth. The only thing is, Mr. Masson, you'll have to move cautiously. When you turn over a stone you never know what you may find under it."

Something in his tone made Hall demand, "Do you know what I'll find?"

"There's no harm in telling you; I understand you inherit so you'll see the figures for yourself. Your brother made some big withdrawals from his account in the last three months. Thirty thousand in all."

"Thirty thousand!" Hall was stunned.

"The only obvious conclusion I could see," the captain said, "was that he was being blackmailed by someone. And I kind of wondered

63

if it was on account of his wife."

"Why?"

"Well, it's a small community. There was some talk that, the day before she died, Mrs. Masson was seen at the Stagecoach Inn, lunching with some guy whom the waiter didn't notice, and she was carrying on and making a big scene."

The captain pushed back his chair. "We'll try to trace the writer of this letter and we'll keep in touch with you. What are your plans?"

"I don't know. I hadn't seen Robin for a long time and he was no letter-writer. Now and then he would call me long distance so we kept in touch. How did he spend his time after he left the army? Who were his friends?"

"Well, he had a lot wrong with him physically in the beginning, of course. After he could get around he started seeing Lillian Halsted. They were always together until they married. A very attractive young couple." As Hall waited expectantly the captain went on, "Sports were out for him and he didn't need a job, of course."

"I can't imagine Robin without a consuming interest. It's not like him."

"Well, he was taking an interest in politics."

"Politics! Robin?"

"Maybe I should say he was taking an interest in a candidate." The captain was carefully noncommittal. "He was the strongest backer Millard Welford had. Welford is running for Congress — that is, if he can get enough names on the petition for his party."

"I remember now. He was a speaker at the memorial service, wasn't he? I remember seeing his name in the newspaper account, but at the time other things —"

"The principal speaker," Gerfind said dryly.

"You don't like him, do you?"

"I don't think I've exchanged a dozen words with him in my life."

"Stop hedging." Hall was impatient. "What's wrong with Welford?"

"I don't like his politics. My people have suffered enough from racism and there's no place for it in New England — if anywhere. Welford is trying to establish a neo-fascist party here."

"You mean Robin was backing a thing like that?" Hall was incredulous. "Robin?"

"As I understand it, your brother's death will be a great blow to Welford's political prospects. Well —" The captain started toward the door.

"What do you know about a girl named Gail Carlyle?"

"She's a newcomer. Librarian. Goodlooker. Her brother, Gregory Carlyle, moved

65

here a couple of years ago with his wife, bought half of that duplex on Maple Street. Three months ago his wife died and his sister came to keep house for him. He's a guy with a hair-trigger temper. He was charged once with assault and battery. The other fellow had been beating a dog so I sort of sympathized with Carlyle."

This time Gerfind walked firmly toward the door.

"Don't try anything on your own. We'll find out who slashed those tires. I don't like that."

Hall laughed. "Neither do I."

"I mean it showed deliberate vindictiveness. Someone has a real grudge against you and he's got a knife."

FIVE

Standing at the living room window Hall watched the State Police car drive away. From here the white obelisk seemed to dominate the Green, to dominate the village. Cars moved in and out of parking spaces along the Green, a trickle of people on foot walked slowly. Already the heat was beginning to be oppressive.

Hall groped for a pipe, lighted it. Lillian had died three hours before Robin. Three hours! For the first time he considered the possibility that Halsted had been right, that Robin had killed his wife and then himself. Three hours to build up his courage? Three hours of hell?

No, whatever had happened, that was impossible. Robin simply could not have killed Lillian. There was no reason for it unless he had lost his mind. Gerfind had implied jealousy. Mrs. Cushing said Robin had taken to watching Lillian anxiously. Frank Burgess had suggested that the Halsteds had spoiled her. The Halsteds themselves — damn it all, the thing didn't make sense. They would never have tried to protect Robin's memory, believing him guilty of their niece's murder, unless — unless they knew or suspected a motive strong enough to justify Robin for killing her. And no motive was that strong.

Hall's thinking had come full circle. He knew too little of Lillian to understand her character, her quality. But Robin? He tried to weigh the possibility with detachment. True, Robin had never been willing to share a girl with anyone else, even a girl in whom he had the most casual interest. But he wouldn't have killed her.

It followed then that he would not have killed himself unless — Hall found himself walking up and down the room — unless he had found Lillian dead and then in grief had destroyed himself. No, that didn't fit with Robin's character. He wouldn't have turned a gun on himself until he had found the bastard who had killed his wife and dealt with him.

Someone had been blackmailing Robin. Thirty thousand dollars. But what in the name of God could Robin have done that would give anyone such a hold on him? Or what had Lillian done? Why had Robin consented to put his popularity and prestige at the service of a small-town Hitler like Millard Welford? Welford of all people.

He recalled Frank Burgess's oblique comment that Lillian's death might be explained by the fact that his aunt had disinherited him. Burgess must know or suspect more than he was telling. But he'd tell, Hall decided grimly.

Something about the pretty living room disturbed him. He couldn't stay in it without conjuring up the picture of the bodies of Robin and Lillian as Mrs. Cushing had found them. He prowled restlessly through the little house from the low attic with its narrow bedroom and storage space to the second floor with its three rooms: the bedroom Robin had occupied as a boy, the larger one he had shared with his wife, and the one which had been used by his aunt as a guest room and which had now been converted into a kind of study for Robin.

Hall went grimly through the papers on the pretty desk in the big bedroom. Lillian had not been a person to surround herself with clutter. There were a few modest bills, some personal and unrevealing letters from school friends, invitations, and a small appointment book. Hall turned the pages without hope or interest. The State Police would not have overlooked this. Most of the entries were cryptic, as Lillian had been given to the use of initials.

She and Robin had been found dead on the morning of June thirtieth. On the twenty-ninth there were two scrawled entries: "Stagecoach 12:30" and "7 — here."

Queer that no one at the Stagecoach had

seen the man with whom Lillian had lunched — and quarreled. Queerer still that no one had come forward to acknowledge dining with the Massons that night.

Robin's study had a businesslike desk and chair but the desk drawers were empty, apparently never used. In a revolving stand beside a big easy chair there were half a dozen books on politics and contemporary history, among which he noticed his own book, *The Faceless Generation.* It was keeping rather odd company. While he had not read all the books, he was familiar with them. Robin seemed to have been steeping himself in some very peculiar doctrines. Odd, Hall reflected, how few people realized that fascist positions were not conservative, not even reactionary; they were as subversive as Communism, as potentially destructive to the whole constitutional fabric. Why had Robin involved himself in the campaign of Millard Welford?

"Oh, here you are," Mrs. Cushing said unnecessarily. "Your lunch is ready. Can you manage about dinner just for tonight? I hadn't expected to stay so I promised to baby-sit for my daughter. It's her wedding anniversary."

"Fine. Just fine. I'll make out all right."

She looked at him sharply. "The weather is telling on you, too. Never knew such a long heat wave. I've fixed you a cold salad and some sandwiches. Oh, your car's been repaired. I guess the State Police put the fear of God into Harry."

Hall didn't need the car to walk the long block to the library. As he passed the white shaft of the obelisk he noticed that there were more fresh flowers.

The ivy-covered library was an old stone building, dark and cool. When Hall's eyes had adjusted from the brilliant sunlight he saw the girl at the desk, absorbed in a book.

"Good afternoon, Miss Carlyle." She was even prettier than he had realized the night before. The deep warm rose of her thin linen dress seemed to be reflected in her coloring. A vivid woman if a hostile one.

She looked at him in silence, apparently bracing herself for trouble.

He put the library book on the desk. "I found this in my brother's bookshelf," he said easily, "and thought I had better return it."

She took it from him, looked at the date and estimated the amount of the fine.

"Quiet in here," he said when he had paid her.

"We try to keep it so."

He noticed that she was endeavoring to shove out of sight the book she had been reading when he came in and he recognized the jacket.

71

"I'm flattered," he said boldly.

She looked puzzled. "It's not at all what I expected."

"What did you expect?"

This time she met his eyes squarely. "I thought you were just another phony." She was aware how deeply she had angered him.

"How you must have hated Robin!"

"I'm not the only one. That obelisk on the Green is a cheat and he knew it was a cheat. I hope it tortured him every time he looked at it, unless his monumental conceit —"

"Hated him enough to put a bullet through his head?" Hall asked, his voice under control. "Enough to put a bullet through Lillian's heart?"

She stared at him. "Are you crazy?"

"Someone slashed the tires on my car last night or early this morning. Someone sent me an anonymous letter warning me to get out of town. I don't scare, Miss Carlyle. You might tell your friends that."

"My friends!" The color drained out of her face. "Are you by any chance telling me the truth?"

He laughed suddenly. "Apparently you would find that a novel experience." He looked around the library. "Is this where you had your noisy quarrel with Lillian, whom you didn't even know?"

Her face was paper white. "You can't talk in here. People are doing research in the stacks."

"But we are going to talk, you know. Will you have dinner with me tonight?"

"Certainly not."

"Then I'll call at your house this evening. It's the duplex on Maple Street." He added casually, "According to the State Police."

"No, you can't go there!" He stood watching her, as though he would stay there forever. Then she said, "I'll have dinner with you."

"Good. I'll pick you up. Seven all right?"

"Seven," she said. She turned her head. "Sorry, Mrs. Graham, it's out but I'll put you on the waiting list."

II

As Hall turned to leave the library he met Burgess coming in. The old man's color was bad but his face lighted up.

"Hall! Were you looking for me? Come downstairs and we'll have a chat. My next boy isn't due for another half hour. Plenty of time."

The basement was cool but airless and Burgess's breathing was difficult.

"Look here," Hall said in concern, "should

73

you try to go out on a day like this?"

"I undertook the job and I intend to see it through."

Hall's protest died on his lips. The old teacher must be eighty, he was obviously frail and defiantly overtaxing himself but there would be no point in protesting. As a teacher Burgess had been a perfectionist who made no allowances, considered no compromises. But he was equally ruthless in dealing with himself.

When his breathing had returned to normal he began to talk eagerly about what he was attempting to do for the boys whose activities he was supervising. He was experimenting to see whether they could be salvaged instead of sent to reform schools. The magistrate was an enlightened man who had agreed to let him try it for a few months.

"Are you succeeding?"

Some of the eagerness died out of Burgess's face. He made an oddly fumbling gesture with his swollen, misshapen hands. It was a long-range project. One couldn't be sure how much one had accomplished. Sometimes he even suspected the boys of lying to him. In an ideal society, of course, the conditions that had molded them would be removed.

"You don't agree with that," he said abruptly.

"Agree that conditions could be improved? Naturally. There's no possible argument about that."

"But?" the old man persisted.

Hall laughed. "Several buts. You want — you've always wanted — a utopian state."

"What's wrong with that?"

"Utopias are always totalitarian in nature. Haven't you noticed that? Your ideal state can exist only under certain rigid conditions to which everyone is expected to conform, for his own good, of course."

"But if people are better off, healthier, happier?"

"Those are the faceless people you're talking about, the ones you've fitted into your own pattern, from whom you've wiped away all individuality. Anyhow, you can't legislate human nature, human impulses. There are such things as genes and inherited tendencies."

"We could control them," Burgess said firmly.

Hall grinned. "I know. It's been tried. Wide-scale conditioning. But in the long run there's no avoiding the bitter fact that we are responsible for ourselves, though we try to escape that knowledge, to fix the blame elsewhere. Pushing guilt onto someone else, something else. Do you remember that quatrain Dr. Johnson once wrote?

How small of all that human hearts endure
The part which laws or kings can cause
    or cure.
Still to ourselves in every place consigned,
Our own felicity we make or find.

By the way, what do you think of this attempt
to establish a fascist party in Connecticut?"

"It's wholly evil," Burgess said promptly.
"A hate party."

"But let's suppose that Welford really be-
lieves in it, as you believe in your ideas. What
do you do then?"

There was a long pause. At last Burgess said,
"You are worrying needlessly, I think. Welford hasn't a chance since —"

"Since Robin died."

"I don't think Robin really believed in those
ideas. In my opinion he was pressured into
exploiting them."

"Pressured? How?"

"You don't understand Robin. He gave all
he had to the war but it took all he was. Perhaps we have just so much stamina and we
can exhaust it as we exhaust everything else.
His nerve was broken, Hall. I could see it in
the little things. I believe he could have taken
that in his stride, though he would have hated

it, but there was the obelisk to live up to. I felt profoundly sorry for him but I honestly believe he was glad to die. He had begun to realize how much harm can be done by stirring up teen-agers, making them feel they are running things, whipping them up into screaming mobs to attack minorities."

"Has that happened here?"

"Only once. But I talked to the owner of the local newspaper and to the troopers. They kept it out of the news, prevented the reporters in other towns from getting wind of it. That disappointed the kids. The whole thing fizzled out like a damp firecracker. It's not likely to happen again. Without Robin's support, Welford's campaign isn't going anywhere. The back of his party has been broken."

"If it hasn't, I'll stay on to help with the good work. Robin was right. Sometimes it's more important to make history than to teach it."

A movement caught Hall's eye and he saw the legs on the circular staircase, blue jeans, scuffed shoes. The boy was listening. Then there was a scurry as he ran up the stairs.

Hall pushed back his chair, ran after the eavesdropper. He wasn't in the library, he wasn't in sight on the street. There was nothing moving but a Volkswagen that was just turning the corner. No point in pursuing him. Anyhow, what harm had been done? None the less, Hall was uneasy.

He looked for the librarian and found her busy at the card index. She hadn't seen anyone, she said indifferently.

"It doesn't matter," he said but he had an irrational feeling that perhaps it did.

III

Even with the windows of the Buick open the car was hot. According to the telephone directory, Millard Welford lived outside the village. The house, at the end of a long dirt road, was modern, with a fine view. At least forty thousand dollars, Hall estimated. Welford must be getting money somewhere. Discreet inquiries had revealed that he was not engaged in any profession, that he had no known source of income. Of course there was limitless money behind the various neofascist parties that were springing up all over the country, invading colleges, arousing teenagers to violence. On the other hand it was possible that the money had come from near at hand, that he had been Robin's blackmailer. Hall was looking forward to meeting Millard Welford again.

The door was opened by a young woman

with a narrow face, observant eyes, and an air of competence. As she recognized Hall, her fingers tightened on the knob. He was aware that he had shocked her out of her composure. While he could have counted five slowly she stood motionless.

Then she flung open the door and held out both hands, smiling brightly. "You must be Hall Masson! I am Freda Welford. How kind of you to come. Millard will be so sorry to have missed you but of course he'll get in touch right away."

Her voice was high and carrying. She drew Hall forward, holding his hand with both of hers, directing his attention by an effort of will toward the view from the glass wall at the end of the living room. Over her shoulder Hall saw a door close quietly.

The room had an impersonal look: two walls of glass, low white couches, lower tables, tube-like lighting, white wall-to-wall carpeting. The only color in the room was an abstract painting of bold patches of red and orange from which Hall hastily averted his eyes.

"I'm so glad now," Mrs. Welford chatted on rapidly, "that Millard insisted on having the house completely air-conditioned. This terrible heat wave. Do let me give you a drink."

She opened a cabinet revealing an impressive array of bottles. "Name your poison."

"Scotch and water."

"Fine. Two Scotch and water coming up." She laughed merrily. Then she sobered. "I'm so sorry. You can't feel much like laughing. Such a terrible, terrible tragedy. Both so young, so much ahead for them. How anyone could have done that! Millard is simply heartsick."

"I understand Robin was backing his campaign."

"He was certainly Millard's most ardent supporter. Like brothers." She saw Hall's expression and faltered.

"What brought about the change? The last time I saw Welford —"

"So he was angry. He had a right to be. You've got to remember that Robin blinded him, that he lost an eye!" Her voice had become shrill. "Do you know what that meant to a young man just ready to start his career?"

"I know exactly what it meant to Welford. Fifteen thousand dollars. I paid him myself. And he started that fight. I saw the whole thing."

"Well —" For a moment Mrs. Welford seemed at a loss. "All that was a long time ago. Water over the dam. And besides —"

"That was in another country and besides the wench is dead."

80

"Wench? There was no girl involved. Just some boyish joking by Millard, saying Robin coasted along on his looks while Millard worked. Though I'm sure, in my opinion, Millard was better looking. More manly."

She stirred uneasily under Hall's unwavering eyes. "Anyhow, they had both forgotten it," she said earnestly. "They became the best of friends. I guess Robin's death is about the worst blow Millard ever had."

"Financially or politically?"

"Well, prestige is really the word."

"How much money did Robin put up for the campaign?"

"Not a cent. Anyhow, Millard didn't need —"

When she did not complete the thought Hall asked, "Have you any idea what was back of those two deaths? How it happened?"

She shook her head. Then her face hardened. "I don't know just what you are after but you can't pin anything on Millard. Not a thing. He is the last person on earth who would have wanted to kill Robin. The very last. Use your head and you'll see how much Robin's support meant. He was the big hero around here. People would believe anything he told them. If he backed a man they would all back him."

"Nothing was said about Robin withdrawing his support that last night at dinner?"

"Not a thing. Oh, they argued some about methods and using —"

"Gangs of boys?" This time he completed the thought.

"I suppose you got that from Burgess. The old man is forty years behind the times. He doesn't realize how important it is to get young people involved in their communities."

"So you were the mysterious dinner guests," Hall said.

"We — I didn't say —" She broke off, hiding her shaking hands behind her. Then her voice rose. "Where are you going?"

"To the State Police. They don't like people who withhold evidence."

She caught up with him, clutched at his arm. "Please! You simply can't build anything on that. Millard will —"

"You can tell him it's safe to come out now, Mrs. Welford. I'm going."

SIX

Gail Carlyle was waiting on the front porch of the duplex when Hall drove up. Before he could get out of the car she was opening the door and climbing in. He didn't fool himself that this indicated any impatience to see him, simply an inordinate haste to get him away from the house.

"As I recall," he said as he put the car in gear, "there aren't any local restaurants. Have you any preference?"

"Wherever you like," she said with a meekness that made him grin to himself.

"Then suppose we try the Stagecoach?"

A few miles beyond Shelton the old pre-revolutionary inn had been restored, with ample parking space outside and a minimum of light inside. There were half a dozen small rooms, each containing a dozen tables, and each with a darkly shaded candle. It was one of those places, Hall saw with resignation, where the menu should be written in Braille. At least he could understand now why Lillian had been able to lunch here with a man whom no one had noticed.

Over martinis he talked easily, speaking of the changes in the village, the things that struck one particularly after a lengthy sojourn in an underdeveloped country. He indicated his glass of water.

"Little things like this, for instance. Water you can trust. The people all looking prosperous and well fed. Oh, I know we have bad pockets of poverty but even at their worst they represent an unattainable dream for most of the world."

"If we can only keep it like that," she said.

Now that he had become adjusted if not reconciled to the dim light he was able to study her. A very lovely woman and tonight, in a sleeveless dress of dull turquoise that molded her body, she made it difficult for him to keep his mind on his job.

"Of course we can't keep things as they are. That's stagnation, eventual deterioration. Change is a part of life. But at least we can determine the direction of the change." Without any transition he asked smoothly, "Why did you quarrel with my sister-in-law the day she died?" He added, as she started to protest, "You were overheard."

"Mr. Burgess, I suppose." She sounded resigned. "Doing his duty, of course."

"It was natural for him to tell me that Lillian was terribly upset that day."

"He would regard it as his duty," she said bitterly, "no matter how much harm it did.

I'd prefer a criminal to a ruthless idealist any day."

"But what harm has he done?"

"He brought you straight to me simply seething with suspicion."

"Actually," Hall pointed out, "you were the one who made the first approach, the one who breathed threats, the one who cast ugly slurs at my brother. And speaking of brothers, why were you so anxious to prevent me from meeting yours?"

"What's wrong with you?" she exclaimed impatiently. "Do you like quarreling for its own sweet sake?"

"But why should I quarrel with your brother?"

She was silent, crumbling a roll.

"Why?" he repeated.

"Keep away from Greg. He's had about all he can take. Three months ago he lost his wife. He was crazy about her and he hasn't been like himself since. It was a terrible shock. She was killed by a hit-run driver. Why are you interested in him?"

"Because you are afraid to have me meet him. The only thing I've heard about him is that he's a guy with a hair-trigger temper and apt to get violent."

"So you thought he had murdered your brother and his wife." She began to laugh.

"If you only knew how funny that is."

"Why don't you share the joke with me?"

"Baiting women amuses you, doesn't it, Mr. Masson?"

"I think you know it doesn't. I believe in any other circumstances you'd be a delightful dinner companion, but for some reason I don't comprehend you have joined the group of people who are determined to keep me from learning the truth about my brother's death."

"And you are determined to find out, whatever the cost."

"Whatever the cost."

While soup plates were removed and steaks placed before them, Hall began to tell her about his brother, younger, gayer, with a quality that attracted friends and cast a kind of brightness around him. His reckless courage had been revealed by his war record. And now, at twenty-five, his life and his promise had been snuffed out.

After a long time Gail said, "War changes people. It's bound to." To his considerable surprise there was a kind of gentleness in her voice. The hostility was gone. "Mr. Masson, I know you were truly devoted to your brother. You would be a happier man if you kept that memory of him intact."

"You think I'll find something to his discredit?"

Her eyes were a clear brown, wide-set and steady. There was pity in them. "I know you will."

"And you won't tell me why you quarreled with Lillian?"

"If it is necessary, but only as a last resort." Abruptly she changed the subject. "When you aren't lecturing and writing and seeking an eye for an eye, what kind of person are you?"

"I hardly know," he said, taken aback.

"What do you play at: music, tennis, sports?"

"Professional sports today don't belong in the sports pages, they belong on the market report. I can't generate any enthusiasm about men who are bought and sold like cattle. I'll settle for the others."

"Good tennis?"

"Only fair."

"What music do you prefer?"

"I never liked that game: 'What book or piece of music would you take to a desert island?' Why narrow an infinite choice? Anyhow, it depends on the occasion. I need Bach to give life its pattern and dignity, and Beethoven its soul. And there are times when I enjoy to the hilt all of Sutherland's pyrotechnics in *Lucia*."

"I'll go along on Beethoven, though I'm still awed by the last quartets. But what's wrong with Haydn? I like a man who has some laughter in him."

Later Hall wasn't sure at what point he had been adroitly maneuvered. All he knew was that he had started out with the intention of taking the Carlyle girl apart and extracting information from her, painlessly if possible, painfully if necessary. He had ended, without quite knowing how, by making a date to play tennis early the following morning.

II

They had sat so long over dinner that there were few cars in the parking lot when they left. He had been right about the intelligence. It leaped to meet his at every point. They talked of books, of foreign travel, of the war in Vietnam, of politics. In a few vigorous phrases she demolished the public image of Millard Welford.

"He's like a figurehead on one of those old ships. Bold-looking but made of papier-mâché. Unscrupulous, ambitious, thinks he's a born leader when he's simply a puppet."

"Whose puppet?" Hall asked.

She shrugged. "They never show their hands, do they, until all the cards are down."

As they pulled out of the parking lot a Volkswagen started up behind them. For a while it followed at a discreet distance, then it passed with a burst of speed and the lights disappeared around a curve. Hall, thinking about the girl at his side and surprised to discover how much he had enjoyed the evening, was vaguely aware of another car that kept some distance behind and made no attempt to pass.

There was something on the road ahead. A dead dog? A deer? Hall stood on the brake, bringing the car to a shrieking halt. The dim bulk on the road was a man, lying at an odd angle, one leg twisted. He wore blue jeans.

Hall pulled the emergency brake and said, "Stay where you are," to Gail. He got out and went to bend over the motionless body. Heart attack? Hit-run?

The body at his feet sprang up like a coiled wire that had been released. At the same time there was a rush of feet and a man closed in from either side of the road.

In that first moment of surprise all Hall had time to see was that they were young and that they were armed with knives. He started to edge toward the hood of the car so that at least his back would be protected. Then he remembered Gail.

He jabbed at the nearest of his assailants and darted off to one side. The boys followed, closed round him.

"Get moving!" he shouted to Gail. "Get out of here."

He didn't have a chance, not against three of them, not against three knives. As he lashed a kick at one of them and felt it connect, a knife slashed his cheek. He felt the blood before he felt the pain. He struck at a moving figure, lunged, hit him in the stomach and another knife flashed. Why the hell didn't she get away?

One of the hoodlums caught his right arm, twisted it behind him, threw him off balance. He fell with one cheek scraping the road. Another of the boys was systematically kicking him over the ribs, over the kidneys. The third flicked a knife and slashed again at his face.

The boys were laughing and Gail was screaming. Then the knife was knocked away, the boy who had held it jerked his head as a fist struck his chin, looked astonished, and crumpled on the road.

"I'm armed," said a harsh voice. "One move out of you punks and you've had it."

There was a flurry of movement, two of the boys picked up the one who had fallen and ran, a motor fired, and a car took off. Someone was pulling Hall to his feet. In spite of himself he grunted with pain.

"Look after the girl. I'm all right."

"Like hell you are. Gail, you drive his car

back, will you? I'll take him with me."

"Greg! Thank God! But how did you happen to be here? Is he badly hurt?" she asked her brother.

"Can't tell but he looks like a mess. I'll get him to the emergency ward at the hospital." He had propped Hall up now and the headlights fell on him. "My God, he resembles Masson, doesn't he."

"He's his brother."

"If I had known before I'd have let them have him. That was my mistake."

III

There seemed to be a number of people doing unpleasant things to him. Then there was nothing at all.

When Hall opened his eyes at last he heard someone say, "Not too bad. A few cuts on his face, some cracked ribs, and a lot of assorted bruises. He'll be uncomfortable for a few days."

He opened his eyes, saw the small hospital room, saw the nurse who was taking his pulse. Uncomfortable, had she said? That was one way of putting it. Every part of his body hurt.

"He's awake now," the nurse said cheerfully, "but don't tire him."

He turned his head to see Mrs. Halsted

standing beside the bed, looking down at him anxiously. He had the curious impression that behind her genuine worry about him there was a sense of profound relief.

"My poor boy! How do you feel?"

He grinned at her. "You heard the nurse. Uncomfortable."

The nurse laughed. "I'll just see about your breakfast." She smiled at Mrs. Halsted and went out.

"How did you learn about this?" Hall asked.

"Miss Carlyle called me the first thing this morning. And, Hall, she sounds like such a nice girl, with a lovely voice. She was awfully upset about what had happened and thought it was time your friends rallied round. She knew Bruce and I were the closest so I came at once."

"Did they get away?"

"Who?"

"That bunch of punks who attacked me."

"I don't know. I haven't heard anything except what Miss Carlyle told me. But she said her brother had reported it to the State Police. What was it all about?"

"That's what I want to know. I have a strong impression they were some of Welford's teen-age punks."

"Millard Welford?" She sounded bewildered. "The man who's trying to start that horrible new party? What has he to do with this?"

"If I'm not mistaken, he is behind it. Organizing young goons seems to be part of his program."

"Do you suppose the State Police can persuade him to identify them?"

"I'd say there wasn't a chance, but I suspect that Mr. Burgess could make a guess about them. He's been attempting to reform some of that lot all summer." He told her about the boy who had been eavesdropping on the stairs when he and Burgess had talked the afternoon before. "I made some comment about staying on here until the Welford party was smashed. If I'm right about this, those boys were also responsible for the slashed tires on my car."

"What's that?"

When he had told her about the malicious mischief and the threatening letter she looked at him in dismay. But again he was aware of her deep sense of relief.

"Mrs. Halsted, has your husband been providing any financial support for the Welford campaign?"

"Hall!" she said indignantly. "Bruce has been a good Republican all his life. Do you think for one single minute he'd get involved with those — those Nazis?"

"I didn't really," he assured her. "But Welford is getting money from somewhere and your husband is probably the wealthiest man in the community. So I had to eliminate him."

"Well, all I can say is don't ever let Bruce know you thought a thing like that about him. It's outrageous."

When the nurse appeared with a breakfast tray Mrs. Halsted left him, to be followed in a few minutes by Captain Gerfind.

The latter grinned at the man on the bed, generally discolored and bruised, with bandages on his head and face, his ribs strapped.

"You certainly stir things up."

"Did you find them?"

"Not yet. All we had to go on was Carlyle's story. A Volkswagen whose color he didn't even notice."

"He couldn't. They'd pulled off the road and there were no lights."

"Three young fellows in blue jeans, armed with knives. Carlyle didn't think he'd ever seen them before and wasn't sure he could recognize them again."

"Probably not. We were fighting out of range of the headlights on my car and he scattered them in a hurry."

"How about you?"

"I doubt if I could pick them out of a crowd

though we were scrapping at close range. It was dark. All I know is that they were all young, long hair, generally unkempt impression." After a moment's pause Hall added quietly, "They meant business, Gerfind."

"What sparked that attack?"

Hall told him about the eavesdropper at the library who had overheard Hall's comment about the Welford organization and who had disappeared before he could catch up with him.

"Come to think of it, there was a Volkswagen moving away then. This isn't evidence, it's just a hunch, but I think they may be a part of Welford's organization. Stupid, belligerent, unable to compete on an equality, the kind that resorts to violence, that finds it courageous to attack a minority, particularly if they are ten to one — and armed."

"Have you any reason for associating them with Welford except for their general type?"

"Well, yes, I have. I've picked up one bit of information for you, Captain. Welford and his wife were the dinner guests at my brother's the night he was killed."

The captain sat up alertly. "Are you sure of that?"

"Positive. Mrs. Welford gave herself away to me."

"What about Welford?"

"While I was at his house our hero was lurking behind a door listening to what we were saying. He never showed."

A slow grin appeared on Gerfind's face and then it faded. "But if they didn't admit at the time that they had been there it might simply be because a man aiming at public life doesn't want to be involved with any scandal. That doesn't seem to be a sufficient motive for killing."

"Welford had a motive. I think Robin was withdrawing his support. At least he balked at Welford's methods. Mrs. Welford let that out, too."

This time Captain Gerfind's grin grew broader. "I'll say one thing, Mr. Masson. You're like your brother in more ways than one. You certainly have a way with women."

"Hasn't he," Gail said as she came into the room with a box of roses.

SEVEN

"I'm sorry about that tennis date," Hall said.

Gail laughed as she settled in the chair beside his bed, crossing her long slim legs. This was the first time he had been able to see her by daylight. A lovely woman, there was no doubt about that, and for once without hostility. Or had she decided to try another method?

"That was your brother who came to the rescue last night, wasn't it?"

"Wasn't it fortunate," she said in her slow voice, "that he happened to be passing by?"

"Somehow I had an odd feeling that he had been behind us all the way from the Stagecoach."

Gail got up to arrange the roses in a vase the nurse had provided. With her back to him she said, her voice as light as his had been, "Now why would Greg do a thing like that?"

"That's what I hoped you would tell me. About all I remember is that he scattered those punks by saying he was armed, and that he seemed to regret the whole thing after he learned who I was."

"He wasn't armed," Gail said quickly. "Greg doesn't own a gun of any kind. That was just a bluff."

"Come here and sit down. I can't talk to the back of your head." Hall waited until she had returned to the chair. "Why was he following us in the first place?"

Gail capitulated. "That was my fault. I'm not much of an actress, I'm afraid. I didn't want him to know I was having dinner with you. He suspected something was wrong and he wanted to know what I was being so mysterious about."

"And why were you being mysterious?"

"I don't like scenes and Greg has a quick temper. He'd have been furious."

"If I may say so, your brother seems to be a rather dictatorial gent. Does he always supervise your dates?"

She got up. "There's really no use, is there? This morning I came here out of gratitude for the way you tried to protect me last night, by drawing the boys off the road so I could get away in safety, though it left you without a chance. I felt — friendly. But you just hammer away and hammer away —"

"One can't hammer at a smoke screen and that's what you keep on creating." Hall moved restlessly and winced.

"You're in a lot of pain, aren't you? You should be resting."

"Don't go." As she hesitated, he repeated, "Please don't go. Somehow I feel that we shouldn't be enemies, you and I."

She gave him a startled look. "I'll see you again before you leave the hospital."

"Before I leave? I'm getting out of here today."

"But you can't."

"Certainly I can. They've patched me up. I don't need to lie in bed while those ribs and the assorted cuts and bruises heal. There's work to be done and not unlimited time in which to do it. I have a deadline to meet on my articles, and a lecture tour starting in November for which I've made no preparation. Sorry to be sordid about it but that's the way I earn my living."

"But you'll have your brother's estate now, won't you?"

"I'd forgotten that. In any case —"

"You're going on with it."

"I'm going on with it."

"You couldn't even drive a car in your present condition."

"I'll manage somehow," he said impatiently. "There's one thing sure, Miss Carlyle; there will be no peace for me or for a lot of people in Shelton until I've seen this thing through."

"Oh, damn!" she said in exasperation. "You're the most stubborn man I've ever encountered. But you simply can't drive yourself. How do you know you won't be attacked again? You couldn't even defend yourself in your present condition."

"So what do you suggest?"

"I'll drive for you if you'll agree to stay here at least one more day."

He was so surprised that he was still gaping at her speechlessly when she opened the door and went out.

In the hall he heard her speaking and recognized Burgess's voice. In a moment the old teacher came in.

"Hall! I've just heard. How are you, my dear boy?"

"A bit battered, that's all. How did you hear about this?"

"I was at Harry's Service Station — he has been splendid about employing my boys, you know — and he told me someone had come in with the news. Millard Welford, I think. You know how things like that get around."

"I'm beginning to. I'm afraid it was some of your boys who attacked me."

"Oh, no!" Burgess was appalled. "There's not a week I don't talk with them. I'd be sure to guess if they were misbehaving."

There was amused affection in Hall's face.

"And why would they do that?" Burgess demanded.

Hall told him of the boy who had been

eavesdropping on the stairs but who had disappeared by the time he got to the library door.

"So that's why you went away so quickly. I wondered." Burgess ruminated, his face troubled. "What were we discussing that the boy could overhear?"

"As I recall, I had just said that I would stay on here to help smash the Welford organization."

"But none of my boys would — that is, whatever mistakes they may have made, they are on the right track now."

"Which of them was due for an appointment at the time when I was talking to you?"

"I don't remember now but I'll look it up. And you couldn't be sure he was involved in that accident of yours if you didn't see his face. We mustn't jeopardize his future by making any unprovable statements."

"But you wouldn't conceal the truth to protect him, would you?"

"Of course not." Burgess was indignant. "If my boys are coming under Welford's influence they must be stopped. But I did hope, with all the summer activities the Halsteds have provided free for young people, and with Harry finding jobs for some of them, things would be all right."

He stood up, a frail but indomitable old

man, bracing his shoulders with an air of decision. "Things must be made right, Hall."

"That utopia of yours." Hall grinned at him. "I'd hate to live in it."

"Would you prefer Welford's inferno?" Burgess demanded with a touch of asperity.

"Before we're done we'll have cut Welford down to size," Hall promised him.

"And just why the hell," Welford demanded as he strode into the room — Welford, as Hall recalled, never merely walked; he strode — "are you gunning for me? Look here, Masson, I don't want trouble; I particularly don't want trouble with you. But when you sic the State Police on me, when you accuse me of blackmail, I'm not taking it. Understand?"

"A child would understand," Hall said mildly. "Perhaps that's an occupational hazard."

"What does that mean?" Welford demanded. A very aggressive-looking fellow, Welford, with his prominent chin, that air of the clean-cut professional athlete.

"Learning to address yourself to the child mind. Keeping it simple so even a fool can understand you."

"I like to talk straight to the people. You want to make things fancy, like Burgess. That's the professor type for you."

"How you must despise what you call the

people," Hall commented.

Welford stifled his angry retort. He chuckled. "Well, here we go again! We never saw things the same way, did we? But live and let live, that's what I say. That's all I ask."

"Moderation itself," Hall said amiably.

"Well, that's what I thought. And what's so funny about that —"

"Welford," Burgess demanded, "what have you been doing with my boys? Last night, according to Hall here, three of them waylaid him and beat him up. Cut him, too."

"Now that," Welford said, his face flushing, "is nonsense. It's slander. It's actionable."

"Nothing to stop you from trying," Hall suggested.

"Look here, Masson, you've never liked me but I'm doing a good job here, a necessary job, and Robin was backing me. What are you trying to do, destroy your brother's own work?"

"Why was he backing you?"

"He believed in what I stood for."

Hall began to laugh uncontrollably and stopped as he felt the sharp pain in his cracked ribs and one of the cuts on his face began to bleed again.

"How much money did you get out of him, Welford?"

"That's what you asked Freda. Not a penny.

Not one single penny. All I asked for was his support, his prestige, and he gave it to me, Masson. Ask anyone."

"Until the night he and his wife were shot. What happened then?"

"You're barking up the wrong tree. I'm the last man on earth to want Robin dead. I can tell you one thing: he might have balked now and then but he'd have backed me right up to the hilt." He gave Hall that direct, man-to-man look which proved so effective when he was making speeches, nodded curtly and went out of the room.

"Sure of himself, isn't he?" Hall said.

"It's true, though," Burgess told him. "I feel sure that Robin would have continued to back him, no matter how much he hated it."

"What leverage did Welford use?"

"That obelisk on the Green. It meant a lot to Robin." The old man got up. "Look after yourself, Hall. Welford sounds like an empty drum but so have other would-be dictators. Don't underestimate him."

"Just the same, I'd be willing to take my oath that the ones who roughed me up last night were his boys," Hall said.

"My boys," Burgess corrected him. His lips tightened. "I'll find out. I won't tolerate having Welford destroy what I'm building up. Good morning, Hall."

When the old man had gone it occurred to Hall that, however different their methods and their objectives, there was a certain similarity in viewpoint between Millard Welford and Frank Burgess.

II

Next morning the hospital room was scented with Gail's roses, now full-blown. Overriding the doctor's protests, Hall managed, with the assistance of an orderly, to get dressed. Shaving proved to be a more difficult matter and started the cuts on his face bleeding again. He insisted on having the large bandages replaced by others as small and inconspicuous as possible, and even then he looked, as he admitted to himself, as though he had had a losing argument with a buzzsaw.

Getting out of bed had required assistance and had been painful but he found that he could walk and, unless he raised his arms or bent over, he could get along reasonably well. In another five to ten years he would probably discover the extent of the internal damage.

He was checking out at the desk in the main lobby when Gail Carlyle arrived, wearing a yellow linen dress that looked crisp and cool and that did justice to her tanned skin and dark brown hair. Even under the tan he could see her beautiful coloring. Like a long-stemmed rose, he thought, and was astonished at himself.

"You weren't going to wait for me!" she accused him.

"I never dreamed you meant it. What about your job?"

"I'm only a volunteer worker at the library and I found someone to replace me." She added with a challenge in her voice, "Indefinitely."

When she had helped him into the Buick convertible and he had settled himself with a grunt, she slid behind the wheel.

"Where first?"

"I'd better stop at the house. I forgot to notify Mrs. Cushing and she may be worried."

"Oh, that's all right. I called her."

"That was thoughtful of you. Then we'll drive to the Stagecoach."

"It's only ten o'clock. They won't be serving now."

"That's what I hoped."

She put the car in gear and turned east. The sky was misty with heat haze and the air was heavy to breathe. The temperature must already be eighty. This was going to be another sweltering day.

When they reached the inn, the parking

lot was empty except for a delivery truck and a few cars that probably belonged to employees.

Hall tried to open the car door and found he could not.

"I'll ask them anything you want," Gail suggested.

"No, I'll handle this."

She went around to open the door and help him out, wincing and stifling a grunt.

The inn was brightly lighted. A man was mopping the floor in the bar, a couple of women were washing tables in one of the small dining rooms, there were raised voices from the kitchen.

A man in shirt sleeves came to say, "We aren't serving yet."

"I want some information," Hall said.

The man looked at him, noticed the discoloration, the bandages on his face, the stiffness of his bearing. Then his eyes widened in recognition. "You must be Lieutenant Masson's older brother. I heard you had come back. Sit down. It was a terrible thing. Anything I can do. Anything at all. Coffee?"

Hall glanced at Gail, who shook her head.

"You've been in an accident," the manager said in concern.

"This," Hall assured him, "was no accident. But that's not why I am here. The day before my brother and his wife were killed, Mrs. Masson was lunching here with some man. She was recognized but the man who accompanied her was not. What I —"

"Mr. Masson," the manager interrupted earnestly, "I'll let you talk to the waiter who served them but he won't be able to help you. The police questioned him; in fact, he came forward in the first place to volunteer the information. I've questioned him. He's done his best to remember. Thing is, this place is kept rather dark; people like eating by candlelight, though I've never understood it myself. I like to see what I'm eating and the food here is worth it."

"I know. I had dinner here night before last."

"So you know." The manager looked pleased. "As a rule we'd be able to recognize people, certainly anyone as prominent as the Massons. But that day there was a convention of some kind, at least it was a luncheon meeting of people interested in historical spots. We were taxed to capacity and our waiters ran themselves ragged. There wasn't time to notice the customers."

"But the waiter did notice Mrs. Masson," Hall pointed out.

The manager called, "Saul, come here a minute, will you?"

A thin waiter, wearing a heavy apron and carrying a towel, came to the door.

"This is Mr. Masson, who wants to know about the man who lunched with his sister-in-law the day we had the historical society here."

The waiter made a despairing gesture. "I just didn't notice him, and that's the God's truth, sir. They had one of those booths in the corner, and I was run off my feet, just about crazy. It seemed like everyone wanted something different and everyone was in a hurry and the air-conditioning had gone off, and what with one thing and another —"

"But you were sure that you recognized Mrs. Masson."

The waiter hesitated. "Well, the fact is that she was crying. Not just a few tears but really sobbing like anything. Right out loud. And arguing, though it didn't sound as though she were getting anywhere."

"Did you hear what she said?"

"She said, 'If that's what you want, I'll pay your debt.' "

"And that's all?"

"That's all I heard. Every single word I heard."

"It couldn't — this man with Mrs. Masson — could he have been Millard Welford?"

"Oh, no," the waiter said promptly.

"How can you be sure, if you didn't see her companion's face?"

"Because Mr. Welford made a speech to the society. He was sitting at the front table in the front room and we had a loudspeaker system set up so he could be heard in all the rooms. No, sir, that's the one person it couldn't have been."

III

At the State Police Barracks a trooper assisted Hall out of the car. The latter's battered appearance seemed to fascinate him.

"Do you want to wait here or will you come in?" Hall asked Gail.

"I'll come in," she said and he looked at her thoughtfully.

Captain Gerfind got up to shake hands. He glanced in some speculation at Gail, eyebrows raised in astonished arcs.

"Miss Carlyle has taken over the driving for me," Hall explained.

"Well, we've found a few things." The captain seemed rather pleased. "We came down hard on Welford and he admitted that he and his wife were the dinner guests the night of the murder. He swears that they left the house early, not later than nine-thirty, and that both the Massons were alive then. That checks with the doctor's estimate of the time of the earliest death. But there's no evidence either way that the Welfords left when they said they did."

"What was your impression?"

"I don't like Welford, as I told you, but he could be telling the truth — for once. After all, he stood to lose by your brother's death. I can't see his party making much headway without the lieutenant's enthusiastic support." Gerfind gave Hall an uneasy look.

"But suppose my brother withdrew his support or threatened to withdraw it?"

"If there's any evidence we'll find it, but who is to be able to swear as to what those four people talked about that last night?"

"So it looks as though Welford could get away with it." Hall's tone was even but the captain looked more uneasy than ever. "Have you been able to trace the source of Welford's income? I'd like to know whether he got Robin's missing thirty thousand dollars."

Gail looked at Hall quickly, her brown eyes wide.

"He deposits three thousand a month. Bank drafts. But he started doing so several months before the lieutenant began to make his withdrawals."

"Can't you find any indication as to where the man's money is coming from?"

"We haven't enough evidence to justify

prying into the source of his income. He has every right to refuse to answer."

"Maybe I can change his mind," Hall suggested.

"You'll end up in the morgue next time, not the hospital," Gerfind warned him. "Leave this to us, Mr. Masson. Anyhow," he went on quickly, seeing the determination in Hall's face, "you can't reach Welford now. He's making a speech at the Founder's Day picnic and he'll stay until he's shaken every hand and kissed all the babies."

"How about those thugs? Can you tie them in with Welford's organization?"

"We have to find them first," Gerfind reminded him. "So far the only description we've had from you and from Mr. Carlyle would fit about sixty per cent of the kids in this community. But it stands to reason there can't be two sets gunning for you; these are probably the same ones who slashed the tires on your car."

"So we are getting nowhere fast."

"I wouldn't say that." The captain brightened. "We've come up with a queer one. Checked on all the people you saw when you got here, the ones who tried to warn you away." His eyes drifted as though by accident toward Gail, drifted away again. "We've found the typewriter on which that anonymous letter was written."

"Good work!" Hall exclaimed.

"What it comes down to is another dead end. The typewriter is in the office of Harry's Service Station."

"Well, I'll be damned!"

"Only thing is," the captain said, "Harry's never learned how to type and the fingerprints on the keys aren't his."

EIGHT

"Now where?" Gail asked.

"You have earned your Girl Scout badge," Hall said. "I am more grateful than I can say. If you will drop me at the next intersection that will be fine."

Gail turned to face him. "What are you up to?"

He shook his head, smiling.

"I am not," she said slowly, "going to leave you. In your condition you couldn't even defend yourself."

He found himself laughing. "Are you, by any chance, a judo expert or have you a secret weapon?"

"I mean it. If you get out of this car I'll follow you."

"There's no sense in getting you involved any deeper. What I'm going to do now is, frankly, quite illegal."

"But that won't stop you, will it?"

"No, it won't stop me."

She was silent for a long time but she made no effort to start the car. A trooper came out of the barracks, looked curiously at them, and then climbed into a police car and drove off.

"Of course," Gail exclaimed. "You are planning to burgle the Welford house while they are away."

"My God, have you taken up mind-reading or is this a demonstration of extrasensory perception?"

She started the car without making any reply. They did not exchange a word until she braked for the steep turn onto the long dirt road that led to Welford's house.

"Hey," he protested, "what do you think you're doing?"

"I'm going with you."

"Oh, no, you're not."

"Then I'll follow you to the door and wait outside."

Hall groaned. "How did I ever get involved with a pestilential woman like you?"

"I involved myself," she reminded him.

"Why?"

She made no answer, her eyes fixed on the narrow dirt road. At length she pulled into the parking place at the Welford house. The door of the garage stood open.

"Both cars are gone," she said in relief. "I suppose the Welfords are taking over the transportation of the widows and the orphans." She came around to open his door and help him out. "Are we going to be cat burglars or do we break a window?"

"You know, I ought to beat the stuffing out of you, woman."

"It's not your fault," she consoled him, "that I caught you in a weak moment. Lead on, Raffles."

Without much hope he tried the door, which was locked, and walked around the house to examine the windows, which, because of the air-conditioning, were closed and immovable.

"An impregnable fortress, that's what this is," Gail remarked, and there was relief in her voice.

"There's no such thing," Hall assured her.

On their second time round he grasped her arm. "I told you so," he said smugly. A basement window was open. "Hey, what do you think you're doing?"

"I'm going to unlock the door for you. There's no use pretending you could get through that window, strapped up the way you are."

"I won't permit it!"

She freed her arm, bent down and then, after peering into the basement, swung her long legs over the sill. A moment later she dropped out of sight.

"All right," she called. "Go round to the door."

By the time he reached it she was opening

it for him. At sight of her triumphant expression he began to laugh. Together they went through the house: the long living room, kitchen, three bedrooms with baths, a room that Welford was obviously using as an office.

"If the evidence is anywhere it must be here," Hall decided, and he sat down at the big desk.

"What are you looking for?"

"Where does Welford's money come from? Who is backing him? What," Hall hesitated, then went on evenly, "what hold did he have on my brother? What association does he have with a gang of teenagers?"

While he started through the papers on Welford's desk, Gail began to search the files.

"Be careful," she warned him, "not to disturb anything."

"I don't particularly mind having him know his papers have been examined," Hall said. "The more worried he gets the more likely he will be to do something impulsive."

"Like having you shot," Gail commented gloomily.

Welford's bankbooks were in the middle drawer of the desk. At sight of the balance Hall gave a low whistle. There was not, however, any co-relation between Robin's withdrawals and Welford's deposits. There was a thick file of speeches at which Hall glanced in distaste. Twenty years earlier, with Hitler the symbol of horror, hatred, and beastliness, there would have been enough here to arouse lynching fever in the people. We don't remember, Hall thought. We don't learn.

It was Gail who turned up the first bit of evidence, a list of names clipped to a document that described, step by step, the training that groups of boys were to receive for the inciting of mobs. The document had been typed on a machine that used a script resembling handwriting. Hall removed the cover from the typewriter beside Welford's desk and saw that it had standard pica type like that used for the list of names.

"Good girl!" He tucked the papers into an inside pocket of his jacket.

The drawers of the desk revealed nothing of interest except for the bankbooks.

"I wonder," he thought aloud, "where Welford keeps his correspondence?"

"Here," Gail said from the files. "I've looked through about a hundred letters. Do you know he keeps copies even of personal letters, notes of condolence, everything?"

"Saving them for his autobiography," Hall suggested.

He got up to prowl the room, glancing, as any inveterate book lover must, at the titles on the shelves. Then he turned idly to look out of the window at the fine view of distant hills. Gail was still going painstakingly through the files, her face intent, and he found himself watching her.

As though aware of his eyes she looked up at him. Slowly, inexorably, a flood of color crept over her cheeks, her throat. Then she returned to the letter she was reading. The paper trembled slightly in her fingers.

For God's sake, Hall thought in amazement, we've fallen in love with each other.

At last she slammed shut the files. "The list was all I could find of any interest." She did not look at him. "Hadn't we better get out of here before we find ourselves in durance vile?"

"I suppose so." He was, he discovered, reluctant to leave the room. Something tugged at his attention. But there had been nothing significant that he could recall. He followed Gail to the door, still with that odd feeling. She opened it and stood looking out at the beautifully kept grounds.

"What magnificent flowers! And how they've managed to maintain a garden this year with no rain defeats me."

"Wait a minute! I've thought of something." He went back quickly to the office, looked at the shelves, reached for the heavy, ornately bound book on the top shelf, grunted with pain as he tried to pull it down.

Gail who had followed him lifted it onto the desk. "What on earth —" she began.

He indicated the title, *Flowers of the World.* "If Welford is a flower lover I'll eat my hat." He examined the book, saw it was a leather-bound filing case, opened it. On top of the papers was a note scrawled in Robin's school-boy hand:

"You can do as you damned please but I won't stand for whipping up mob hysteria. I'm through and that's final. Tell the whole God damned world what you want to about me. This is it."

Underneath, in a bold clear script, was written: "Called Masson. We'll have dinner there tonight. I'll bring him around."

II

Only when the car had emerged from the dirt road that led to the Welford house and had turned toward Shelton did Gail risk a glance at Hall. What she saw in his face checked the words on her lips. Whatever he had read in the note he had taken with him had had a shattering effect.

"Burgess said he believed that Robin was glad to die." The words seemed to have been wrenched out of Hall's white lips.

Gail concentrated on her driving. Whatever the shock of revelation she had experienced when Hall's look had brought the blood burning into her face she was aware that, for this moment, at least, he had forgotten it, forgotten her. All the comments, whether heated or tactful, that she had been prepared to make, were unnecessary now. She was aware of a curiously letdown feeling and was ashamed. And she was afraid. What had been in the note? What had Hall learned? And what was he going to do about it?

She glanced at her watch and then drove into Shelton and along the Green. She passed the library, turned the corner and went into a driveway. Then she came around to open the door for Hall.

"What are you up to now?" he asked with an attempt at lightness.

"It's nearly one-thirty and I'm starving. I'm going to fix us some lunch."

"I should have thought of that. I've been very inconsiderate."

She helped him out and led the way to the duplex. The half owned by the Carlyles had been furnished in early American, the wide floorboards gleamed with wax, the furniture was satiny with polish.

"Martinis all right, or would you prefer something else? Greg has bourbon, sherry, and beer. That's about all."

"Well —"

She looked at his haggard face. "I'd pre-scribe a martini. You've about had it." She eased him into a chair and went into the kitchen, where he heard her empty an icetray.

He leaned back in his chair. Every part of his body ached and he felt unbearably tired. As Gail had done both the driving and the housebreaking he had not exerted himself much. In fact, looking back, he seemed to have played an ignominious part in the lawless expedition and he had also permitted her to take risks that were unpardonable. As a rule he was capable of detachment but at the moment he regarded himself with considerable distaste.

There was a small table beside his chair on which there was a framed photograph showing two people: a dark young man and a laughing woman. She wasn't pretty but she had a wide, generous mouth and steady, candid eyes.

"That's Greg and his wife Martha," Gail said and set a tray on the table. She poured martinis into chilled glasses and pushed one within Hall's reach. They sipped the cocktails in companionable silence. Then she refilled his glass and went into the kitchen. When she returned she set up small tables and brought their lunch on trays.

They ate in silence. At length Hall said, "It

occurs to me that I've been behaving badly. But I am truly grateful, you know."

"You don't owe me any gratitude." She leaned back in her chair, long slim legs stretched out, a cigarette in her hand. "I started on this expedition of yours to keep an eye on you, to find out what you were doing."

"I guessed that."

"Didn't you mind?"

"There was nothing I wanted to hide," he pointed out. "In fact, I've been at some pains to make my intentions as widely known as I could. Anyhow" — he smiled at her suddenly — "it doesn't really matter, does it, how or why you started out? We're together in this now."

She got up rather hastily to clear away the trays. For a few minutes she was occupied in the kitchen. When she returned he held out his hand.

"Gail?"

She faced him, leaning against the back of her chair as though it were a kind of barrier.

"Gail," he said and this time it was no longer a question. She came toward him slowly as he pulled himself out of the chair. As his arms reached for her she held him off, her hands against his chest.

"Don't," she told him. "You're making a

terrible mistake."

"Am I?" His tone was gentle but there was a glint of humor in his eyes.

"You don't know what you are going to find."

"I've found you."

"That is impossible, Hall. I — wish it weren't, but that's the way it has to be."

"Because of that quarrel you had with Lillian?"

She went back to her chair and sat down. "That's part of it. I don't know what you learned at the Welford house but I've learned something today. We're all guilty — in a way — for those two deaths. We all need to be forgiven as well as to forgive. The Furies were — have you ever thought of them as the Greek version of the Old Testament? And the Eumenides, the Compassionate Ones, as the Greek New Testament? The beginning of civilization. The sunlight after the darkness."

Hall's answer, which was no answer, took her aback. "Why haven't you ever married, Gail?"

"Well, first there was my mother who was an invalid. Then — I was engaged once but I — we didn't have enough in common, I suppose. We were in love but not the way Greg and Martha were, just a kind of infatuation that burned out. Tom didn't agree with me at the time but he is married now so it worked out all right for him."

"And for you?"

She looked at her watch. "It's nearly three o'clock. If you want any more chauffeuring today you'd better get moving. Greg will be home by five."

He sighed. "Are you always businesslike?"

"Always," she said firmly.

He made no comment but the corners of his lips quirked upward. "Then back to the salt mines. Let's take a look at that list you found in Welford's files."

Together they went over it. "Do these names mean anything to you, Gail?"

She shook her head.

"Then we'll consult Mr. Burgess and see whether any of them are his boys. We won't need the car to go round the corner to the library. Actually, I can manage this trip by myself."

"I'm going along," she said firmly and again he gave her a searching look.

The substitute librarian looked up in surprise as Gail passed her with a nod, assisting a much-battered man to descend the circular staircase.

Burgess sat at his desk, talking earnestly to a teenager who listened respectfully. His air of injured innocence was somewhat marred by a discolored lump on his jaw.

". . . absolute confidence in you," Burgess was saying in his gentle voice. He became aware of Gail and Hall, but the boy had seen them at once and looked as though he'd like nothing better than flight. Leaning negligently against the curved railing of the staircase, Hall effectively barred the way.

"All right, Max. Next week at the same time. And don't let anyone else lure you into a fight. Remember that I am responsible for you."

"Yes, Mr. Burgess," the boy said meekly, edged away from the desk and came face to face with Hall, who looked at the bruise on his jaw and then stepped aside to let him go up the stairs.

"Who was that?"

Burgess, with a fussy gesture, got up to offer Gail the extra chair and to greet Hall. "That was Max Brenner, one of my boys."

Hall pulled out the list, ran down the names and nodded. "Uh-huh, I thought so. He's one of the three who set on me with knives night before last, the one Mr. Carlyle knocked out."

"Oh, surely not. Surely not!" Burgess clucked like an agitated hen. "He explained that bruise to me. Some boys set on him. He couldn't help himself."

Hall put down the list. "Anyone else here

whose name you know?"

Burgess ran down the list rapidly. "But I know all of them. Those are my boys, Hall."

"Those," Hall told him grimly, "are the nucleus of Welford's teen-age troublemakers." He silenced the old teacher's horrified protests by laying on top of the list the pages of instructions that had been clipped to it.

When Burgess had read them slowly he looked up at Hall. "Where did you get hold of this extraordinary and disgusting document?"

"I stole it from Millard Welford's files," Hall told him coolly.

Burgess blinked at this bald and lawless statement. Then he replied with equal coolness, "There are times, of course, when the ends justify the means."

"I wonder. By the way, who was the boy on the stairs the other day who overheard our conversation?"

"I checked that up. He is Bill Welling. I see his name is here, too. This thing has got to be stopped. But the boys must be salvaged and not sabotaged. Leave it in my hands."

"I'm sorry, sir, but this situation has got a bit beyond that point, hasn't it?"

"What do you intend to do?" Burgess's purplish lips were shaking.

"Leave it in Captain Gerfind's hands. He's

an honest cop and a very decent man. It's not Welford's tools he is after; it's Welford himself and his backers."

"What do you think he'll do?"

"I hope that he gives all the publicity he can to this set of instructions for the care and feeding of gangs."

Burgess's face brightened. "That," he declared, visibly cheered, "ought to cook Welford's goose."

"Or at least light a fire under it," Hall agreed.

"Will you leave these papers with me? Let me see Gerfind myself. I'd like at least an opportunity to put in a word for my boys."

"Just as you please so long as you keep this stuff safe. It's dynamite. By the way, what is Harry's part in all this?"

"The garage man, you mean? He has been very helpful, offered to give my boys jobs as long as they did their work properly and kept out of trouble."

"What's in it for him?" Hall demanded crudely. "If Harry is a public-spirited citizen I'll never trust my judgement again."

"But that's just it." Burgess pressed his hands together as he had done years before when he launched into a lecture. "Harry was an underprivileged boy who wasn't held in much esteem, but he's a natural mechanic. He began to do well and then he married one of the Matthews girls. You remember them? That big Colonial house with the black shutters. Old family. They were furious about it but the marriage seems to be sound in spite of all the opposition. So Harry wanted the approval of people like his wife's family. He gives a lot to charity, heads civic groups, all that."

"How long has he owned that garage? It looks brand new to me."

"It opened just a week ago. He had another place out of town somewhere but I think he sold it in order to get this one. Bigger, more equipment, able to handle all kinds of repairs. Anyhow, his heart was set on establishing himself in Shelton. A need to prove himself, I suppose."

"Just a week ago," Hall said. "Quite an investment, isn't it?"

"I don't really know about these things." Burgess peered around Hall. "Come down, John. I'm ready for you. Sorry I can't give you more time now, Hall. If there's anything else I'm always home in the evenings."

"There's one other thing. About Robin."

"Can it wait?"

"Yes, it can wait." Hall toiled slowly up the stairs behind Gail.

"Haven't you had enough for one day?" she

asked. "You look so terribly tired."

"I'm not tired. But there's something horribly depressing about turning over stones, isn't there?"

When she made no reply he said, "You gave me fair warning, didn't you? You said I wouldn't like what I found."

"Where are you going?" she asked as he touched his hat and started down the library steps to the street.

"Harry's Service Station. That public-spirited citizen is beginning to interest me greatly."

"I'm going with you."

"No," he told her, "this is one thing I'm going to do by myself."

NINE

Gail tucked her hand under his arm. "Somehow, you don't strike me as being the kind of man to use violence on a woman."

"It depends on the provocation. You're a persistent wench, aren't you?"

They walked slowly along the Green where the grass was turning brown for lack of rain, where the leaves of the maple trees hung limp and lusterless under the sullen and relentless sun. Now and then a rare pedestrian — Shelton, like most American towns, was a place where no one walked except in a dire emergency — spoke to Gail and stared at Hall's battered face.

"Everyone in the village," she predicted, "will call me this evening to ask about you."

"And the moral of that is —"

"I know. Never speak to strange men. I was very nicely brought up, Mr. Masson."

"A young lady," he told her solemnly, "should always be accomplished. Now take your talent for house-breaking."

"Just a natural gift," she said modestly.

They were laughing when they walked into the small office of Harry's Service Station. An oscillating fan stirred the hot air without cooling it. Harry, his shirt sleeves rolled up above his elbows, revealing muscular and unexpectedly hairy forearms, was busy at the telephone.

"But he didn't recognize you? . . . Okay, tomorrow you'd better report at the other shop . . . Until further notice. Jake went down this morning . . . Damn it, you got yourself into this! You'll play it my way or you're out. That clear?"

He slammed down the handset and leaned back in his chair. For the first time he noticed that he was not alone. Something like dismay appeared on his face. Then his fingers went up to cover his scarred lips.

"Looks like you've had an accident, Mr. Masson." The garage man took in every detail of Hall's appearance, the discoloration, the bandages, the stiffness of his carriage as a result of the heavy strapping.

"You warned me, didn't you, Harry? Told me to get out before I got hurt?"

"You don't think I had anything to do with that?"

"I think you could put your hand on the boys who were responsible."

"Now look here, I've been employing some kids this summer, trying to straighten them out, make men of them. No one gave me a hand when I was a kid, I can tell you that, and the youngsters know they can't work for me if they get themselves in trouble. You aren't going to smear me. This is my town. Some day I'm going to be the biggest man in it and I'm going to play it straight." There was a passion, a convincing air of sincerity about him that puzzled Hall.

"Let's take it from my point of view," he suggested. "You warn me to get out of town. Someone sends me an anonymous letter carrying the same message, and that letter was written on your typewriter."

"That's what Gerfind tells me and I was sore as hell about it. I can't even type. The boys write my business letters and type up the bills and all like that."

"Did Gerfind take the boys' prints?"

"They didn't match, not any of them. I suppose someone could have got in here to use the typewriter."

"Did you tell the captain that the boys you have around here aren't the same ones you had yesterday?"

Harry blinked. "He knows that they come and go. We can't make them work if they don't want to. Any work they do is all to the good. Keeps them out of trouble."

"I don't know how you define trouble. These boys slashed the tires on my car; they attacked me night before last with knives. If it hadn't been for the timely arrival of Miss Carlyle's brother I'd have been in real trouble."

"He was in real trouble!" Gail exclaimed. "They nearly killed him."

Harry looked from one accusing face to the other like a baited animal. Then his lips moved in their distorted grin.

"So Mr. Carlyle came to the rescue!" The grin expanded. Harry began to chuckle. "Now that's really something! Picturesque Shelton at its friendly best."

"Let's go," Gail said abruptly.

"Are you helping Mr. Masson in this — uh — crusade of his?" Harry did not attempt to conceal his amusement.

"I didn't come here to discuss Miss Carlyle," Hall said.

"Why did you come?" Harry was feeling sure of himself now; all the insolence was back in his voice.

"I wondered where you got the money for this nice new service station."

"So that's it!" Harry sat quite still, the scars showing on his face. Then he got up. "Why don't you ask the Carlyles, since they're so helpful? You're meddling, Masson; stirring up mud. Stinking mud. I haven't anything else to say to you. Get out of here and stay out. But this much I'm telling you. I didn't kill the lieutenant. I don't know who did. Try to pin that on me and —" He checked himself, added hastily, "I'm not threatening, understand that. Mess around all you like. Stir up the village. But the lieutenant wouldn't thank you for your interference."

II

Mrs. Cushing rushed to the door as Hall walked wearily up the gravel driveway.

"I called the hospital this morning and they said you had insisted on checking out, though you weren't well enough to do it. I've been out of my mind with worry."

Under the insistent pressure of her flurried ministrations, Hall found himself lying on the couch in the living room. The room had been darkened and it was pleasantly cool. For a few minutes he lay with closed eyes, conscious only of his exhaustion and of muscles he'd never been aware of before. Then he was roused by the tinkle of ice and saw that the housekeeper had mixed a pitcher of martinis and had placed a filled cocktail glass beside him.

"I made them just the way the lieutenant used to," she told him anxiously. "Dinner won't be ready for at least three-quarters of an hour. I'm going to have a soufflé, something light because it's such a hot night. You just lie there and rest."

At first the effort to move, to lift the glass, seemed too difficult. After the second sip Hall began to revive, to attempt to sort out his thoughts, to review the day's findings.

He groped in his pocket for the defiant, revealing note that Robin had written to Welford. Robin, as Burgess had implied, had broken under the strain. There was something in his background so ugly that he had surrendered to Welford's pressure and had been blackmailed to keep it hidden. And for the last months of his life he had had to look out on the mockery, the torment, of the obelisk.

Hall was not aware of any feeling of criticism, of condemnation. He had always accepted Robin, his weakness as well as his charm, a human being, fallible but endearing. Now his first feeling was one of pain for Robin's suffering as he had tried to live up to his obelisk.

Welford had tightened the screws. And then, thank God, Robin had rebelled, had preferred to take his medicine than to continue to aid and abet. And yet — and yet — there was no evidence that Welford had received the blackmail money. Welford had needed Robin's prestige to camouflage his fascist policies. Welford, to judge by his bank deposits,

136

was the recipient of far more money than there had been at Robin's ready disposal. But if he were not the blackmailer, there was not proof that he was not the murderer.

Hall refilled his glass. How would a man like Welford react when Robin balked at the idea of gang violence to stir up racism? Would he go to the length of killing? True, the backers of neo-fascist organizations did not appear to have any strenuous objection to murder. Still —

Hall fumbled for his pipe, feeling the heavy tape pull on his sides. In any case, Welford had not been Lillian's lunch companion. He had been very much to the fore, addressing the historical society in what was, no doubt, his own peculiar distortion of American history.

If that's what you want, I'll pay your debt. Those were the only words the waiter at the Stagecoach had heard Lillian speak. It followed, didn't it, that she had lunched with the blackmailer? Something stirred in Hall's memory. Robin had never shared a girl with anyone else. Mr. Burgess had said that Lillian was spoiled. Mrs. Cushing said Robin had taken to watching her anxiously. What the hell did the Halsteds know that they were determined to keep from him? Their own niece killed and they didn't want her murder cleared up. Was it, then, Lillian's reputation that Robin had been blackmailed into shielding?

Hall muttered to himself and went over his interview with Captain Gerfind and its follow-up in Harry's Service Station. That Harry had been hiring Welford's boys was a certainty, but that he had become aware of the extracurricular activities of the boys was less certain. There was a fierce determination in Harry to acquire standing in his community. And he had been amused because of the cooperation between Gail and Hall, particularly amused that Hall had been protected from the hoodlums by Gregory Carlyle. Gregory Carlyle, recent widower, and Lillian. Could that be the missing piece of the puzzle?

Hall finished his second cocktail, puffed at his pipe. One of the cuts on his cheek was beginning to burn. His lower back, where he had been kicked the hardest, hurt damnably. Tomorrow he'd have to see the doctor again. If he were more comfortable he might be able to think more clearly.

Harry had implied, more than implied, that it was Gail who knew the answer to the blackmail, and Gail was afraid to have him meet her brother. He recalled Carlyle's bitter words when he had learned the identity of the man he had saved.

So far it was a three-way chance. The blackmailer could be Harry, with his shiny new garage; Gregory Carlyle, with his inexplicable hostility toward Hall; or Gail herself. And the hell of that is, Hall acknowledged to himself, I'm in love with her. I'd marry her tomorrow, like a shot, if she'd have me.

The telephone rang and Mrs. Cushing left the kitchen to answer it.

"I'm sorry you can't speak to Mr. Masson just now . . . Yes, he's here but he's resting . . . Well, really there's no call to speak to me like that."

"I'll take it," Hall called, and hoisted himself up and off the couch with a grunt. He took the phone from Mrs. Cushing. "This is Hall Masson speaking."

"You bastard!" The voice was rough with fury but Hall recognized it as Millard Welford's. "Breaking into my house. Going through my papers. I'd like to smash your face!"

"What are you talking about?"

"Don't give me that. I know exactly what's missing. What's more I'm going to report to the police."

"In the morning," Hall said, "the stuff will be turned over to Captain Gerfind and I'm going to suggest that those interesting instructions on how to whip up a mob be given the widest possible publicity. Whether you know it or not, Welford, your goose is cooked." He broke the connection and, at Mrs. Cushing's anxious suggestion, went to tackle the soufflé before it fell.

III

Mrs. Cushing had left for the night and Hall, having mixed himself a nightcap, returned to the living room. For a long time he stared down onto the Green where the obelisk soared, white and serene. What a hell of a thing to live with! What was it old Burgess had said? Robin was glad to die. Robin who had throbbed with life. Robin in whom something had snapped when he came to the end of his physical and moral endurance.

Had Robin really killed Lillian and shot himself? To whom had Lillian said, "If that's what you want, I'll pay your debt"? Why had she quarreled with Gail?

But the question that loomed largest in Hall's mind was what had happened during the three hours that had elapsed between Lillian's death and Robin's. Robin had not called a doctor or the police. There was no evidence of a struggle. What had happened?

Someone rang the bell and then, without waiting, hammered impatiently on the door. Hall set down his highball glass and went quietly into the foyer where he switched on the outside light. He wasn't going to be taken unaware a second time by a gang of young goons armed with knives.

There was only one person on the doorstep, a dark, scowling young man. Hall released the bolt and opened the door.

"Good evening, Mr. Carlyle. Glad to see you. Come in. I wanted —"

Gregory Carlyle stood in the doorway, jaw set, angry eyes fixed on Hall under frowning brows.

"I came for just one thing. Keep away from my sister. I mean that, Masson."

"Why?"

"I won't have her involved in your dirty schemes."

"I think," Hall said evenly, "you'll find she involved herself."

"You've got to stop it and stop it now."

Gregory Carlyle had the same look of alert intelligence that characterized his sister but he lacked her unhurried poise. He was like an awakening volcano. He had ill-tempered eyebrows and angry eyes. He might easily be dangerous.

"How?" Hall asked. "I've tried everything I know to stop her."

"Not everything." The volcano was rumbling now.

"She's not doing this for me, you know. She made that clear. And I might suggest that it would be wiser to tackle Gail instead of me."

"Gail? Very friendly for so short an acquaintance."

"It's all on my side," Hall assured him. "I've fallen in love with your sister, Carlyle. You might as well know that now."

For a moment the two men looked at each other. Then Carlyle used the same words his sister had spoken, this time in a curiously deflated, almost bewildered tone. "That is impossible." He went out, closing the door behind him. Hall heard a motor start, heard tires crunch over the gravel driveway.

He went up to bed, undressed slowly and with difficulty, searched the medicine cabinet in the Massons' bathroom. There was a half-empty bottle of sleeping pills. The prescription, Hall noticed in surprise, had been made out to Robin. He took two and went back to his own room.

For a little while he thought of that curious interview with Gregory Carlyle. *That is impossible.* Why? In God's name, why?

Hall turned carefully and painfully, damning the boys who had kicked him. He'd never be able to sleep. He turned again, the pillow slip cool against his cheek, and fell asleep.

IV

He was choking. The volcano had erupted and scalding lava poured toward him. He tried to run, to escape the stream of fire and death that pursued him, but his feet would not budge. He had had that dream before, tried to run with feet too heavy to lift, but never before had he felt this sense of urgency.

He choked again, smelled smoke, tried to rouse himself, but the effort was too great. If he could only breathe without coughing —

The night was filled with sound, sirens, clanging of bells, the throb of motors. Someone was banging on the door. Why, Hall thought dimly, didn't they let him alone? A man had a right to be alone. Somewhere there was the noise of breaking glass. A voice shouted, "Masson!"

Hall's eyes closed and the clouded impressions were swallowed up in darkness.

There was an odd moment when he seemed to be moving upside down. There was a sheet of flame, a blast of heat, shouts. Someone was hurting him unbearably, kicking his broken ribs again. Then he was sick and at last he drew air painfully into his lungs.

He opened his eyes. He was lying on his

back on the lawn. Harry Wilkes, who had been bending over him, sweat streaming down his scarred face, gave him a broad grin and straightened up.

"He's come out of it," he called. "Masson is all right."

Hall turned his head. Flames were shooting out of the roof of the Cape Cod house. Men were moving about purposefully, dragging heavy hoses. Beyond the fire engine was a motley array of vehicles: Cadillacs, jeeps, pickup trucks, Chevrolets, Pontiacs, the cars of the members of the Volunteer Fire Department.

"What happened?"

"Someone seems to have thrown an incendiary bomb at the roof. The Williamses saw the flames and called the fire department. Then they tried to reach you by phone but you must already have been out from the smoke."

"Who got me out?"

"I broke a window," Harry said, "and hauled you down here. Thought you were a goner for a while."

"Well," Hall said awkwardly, remembering their last heated argument, "thanks very much."

"Think nothing of it. Some day," Harry said, unsmiling, "you can do as much for me.

If you're sure you're all right I'd better lend a hand."

"I'm so glad you're all right. We were awfully worried." Hall looked up at the woman who smiled down at him, a heavy-set woman in her middle forties with a pleasant, undistinguished face. "I am Cora Williams, your neighbor. My husband is around somewhere, helping, but I do hope he'll stay off the ladders. He has dizzy spells."

As Hall tried to get up she leaned over. "Pull yourself up on my arm. My husband calls me Powerful Katinka. It's all right."

To his surprise he was able to get to his feet with her help, though there was one difficult moment when they nearly toppled to the ground together.

Now Hall could observe the extent of the fire, the disciplined activity of the men. On the street a mob of curious people watched but without attempting to get in the way of the fire fighters.

"Looks as though the whole place will go," he commented.

"That boy ought to be strung up by his thumbs!" Mrs. Williams exclaimed. "To cause that much damage deliberately — to risk your life — why if it hadn't been for Harry Wilkes — and I'm so glad it was Harry — maybe more people will start being nice to him now

— and that girl he married, too."

Hall sorted this out patiently. "Do you mean that you really saw someone start this fire, Mrs. Williams?"

"Yes, I was looking out and saw him under that street light by the mailbox, right at the entrance to our driveway. He took something out of his pocket and fiddled around with it and then came right here. He acted — it was the way he looked around — anyhow, I watched him and he threw the thing at your roof. I thought it was a rock and then there was a kind of little puff — and then a flame shot out."

"Would you recognize this boy again?"

"Why, of course," she said in surprise. "That street light is much too bright. I've always said so. I could see his features and even his expression. Just as clear as the night young Mrs. Masson died. She came running out about ten o'clock to drop a letter in the mailbox. She was crying. I always wondered, you know, if she had a kind of premonition about what was going to happen."

TEN

"Are you sure about that?" Hall asked at length.

"Oh, quite sure. As soon as you feel up to it, Mr. Williams and I want you to dine with us and then you can see for yourself."

"It seems odd to me that no one has acknowledged receiving that letter."

"Do you think it's important?"

"It might help solve their murders."

"You don't say!" Mrs. Williams, essentially kind, could not resist a vicarious thrill at finding herself, even remotely, associated with the most dramatic crime Shelton had ever had. "Of course, you know the child was upset that day. Usually the sunniest thing, running back and forth from the Halsted house to her cottage, singing to herself, always smiling. But that morning she had a terrific quarrel with Mr. Halsted. They had always been so devoted, you know. Never any trouble. I wouldn't have known about it except I was in my garden and they were on the lawn at the Halsted place. They were arguing like anything. Then she screamed, 'You'll be sorry!' and she ran back to her cottage. Such a pity, you know, to part in anger when it's for the last time."

Someone touched Hall's arm and he turned to find Captain Gerfind beside him.

"Whatever stone you turned over this time, it really started a landslide," he said dryly. "I suppose you know you're lucky to be alive."

"I didn't start the fire. Mrs. Williams here saw it done."

Leaving the delighted Mrs. Williams to her moment of importance, Hall watched the fire fighters. One thing was obvious. The house was going. All that could be done was to contain the fire as much as possible in order to keep it from spreading.

"No wind, thank God," a man muttered as he went past. "One spark could ignite the whole village; the place is as dry as tinder."

Every now and then flames shot skyward from the billowing smoke. Little by little they stopped and the air was thick with the acrid smell of damp, charred wood.

"God bless my soul!" Burgess exclaimed. "What's happened? I was just walking past —"

"At midnight?"

"I don't sleep much. Afraid I do a lot of prowling. It wasn't until I saw the people and the cars that I realized there was a fire. You aren't hurt, Hall?"

"Harry got me out or I'd have died in there."

Burgess beamed. "Harry! How splendid of him. But it looks as though you'd lose the house."

Hall nodded. "I've just been thinking that it's as well I turned that list over to you or there would be no evidence against Welford. Gerfind is here now, by the way, if you want to give it to him."

"I left it at home. Hall, suppose those boys are innocent. Imagine the harm —"

"It was a boy who threw the incendiary bomb at the roof. Mrs. Williams saw him and she'd know him again. And there's no one but Welford who would want that evidence destroyed tonight."

"Then," the old teacher said grimly, "something must be done to stop this evil. I'll go get the list now."

"As long as it is safe it can wait until morning. Anyhow, there's the police car going off. Even policemen have to sleep."

"That reminds me. Where are you going to sleep, Hall?"

Hall looked ruefully at the gaping roof, the burned-out shell of the Cape Cod cottage. "I have no idea." He began to laugh. "There's one thing sure. I can't expect to be taken in at a motel in my pajamas. In fact, until some clothes are found for me I can't appear any place. Besides, my wallet, my traveler's checks, everything has, literally, gone up in smoke."

There was a general roar of motors as cars began to move off and the crowd dwindled away.

"There's Mr. Halsted," Burgess said, and Hall turned to see him hurrying across his lawn, wearing a dressing gown over his pajamas.

Hall watched him approach. For the first time he wondered why it had not been Halsted, who lived next door, who had given the alarm. Just how possible was it that no one at the Halsted house had heard the sirens, seen the flames, smelled the smoke?

"What happened? Good God! Are you hurt, Hall?"

"The fire was set deliberately. Fortunately for me, someone dragged me out and got me breathing again."

"This is a terrible thing. You must come home with me, of course. Dear me, you haven't even any bedroom slippers."

"My rescuer couldn't think of everything. Except my life. Except my life. Except my life."

"In a way, I'm glad the place is gone," Halsted said. "If ever a house had a curse on

150

it — Come on. Come on."

Mrs. Halsted, wrapped in a drab gray robe, was standing on the porch. When her husband appeared with Hall in tow, barefooted, his pajamas scorched where they had brushed the flames in Harry's dash for safety, she cried out in horror.

While she made up a bed in a guest room — their couple had been given a week's vacation, she explained — Halsted, over Hall's protests, called his doctor. Once in bed he fell asleep at once and roused only fitfully while the doctor poked and prodded and made disparaging noises. Then he felt the prick of a needle.

It was midday when he became conscious of the smell of coffee and opened his eyes. Mrs. Halsted was standing beside his bed, a tray in her hands.

"I'm sorry to have to waken you but Captain Gerfind is here and the doctor promised to call again at one o'clock."

"I'm being a terrible nuisance," Hall said. "I don't seem to remember even going to bed."

"Bruce helped you. And that reminds me, he went out this morning to get you some clothes. He'll be back shortly. Meantime he left his dressing gown but I'm afraid — you are so much larger than he is —"

She set down the tray. "If you want anything just ring. I'll leave you to breakfast in peace."

There was barely time for a sip of the scalding coffee before Gerfind came into the room.

"Well, Sherlock," he said cheerfully.

"Don't hit a man when he's down." As the captain laughed Hall said suspiciously, "You look awfully damned pleased with yourself for a man who was up most of the night."

Gerfind sat down beside the bed. "I've been in the Masson murder case for close to a month and, aside from the two queer things I told you, I haven't turned up a damned thing. Then you come along and set the village on its head. You get your car damaged, you get roughed up by a gang, you get your house burned down. But you find out who those elusive dinner guests were the night of the murders, and now you've turned up that list of Welford's hoodlums and the instructions for inciting to riot. Burgess brought them to me first thing this morning. How the hell did you come across that stuff?"

Hall grinned at him. "As a man who likes to keep on the right side of the law —"

"Okay," Gerfind said hastily. "Better not tell me. But if Welford guesses —"

"Oh, he knows. He called last night, mad enough to kill."

"Mad enough to burn down a house?"

"Easily, I should think. And Mrs. Williams —"

"She's a good witness. Long-winded but clear. We'll find that boy for her and I think we'll find him on Welford's list. By the way, Burgess was fighting mad. He said something about publicity. In my opinion, the less said about those instructions the better for all concerned."

"I don't agree with you." Hall lifted the tray to one side. "I'd like to see them in all the news media in America. A secret weapon is no good once it has been revealed. When people understand just what men like Welford are up to, what methods they are willing to employ to accomplish their beastly objectives, they are going to raise Cain."

After a moment a grin spread slowly over Gerfind's face. "Well, now," he said thoughtfully. "Well, now," he repeated in a tone of decision. "I suppose I ought to lock you up for your own protection. Maybe the Halsteds can keep you quiet for a day or two. At least you'll be safe here."

He was followed by the doctor who examined Hall carefully, looking at his cuts and bruises, and lightened the strapping over his ribs. He was not a man who bothered to cultivate a soothing bedside manner.

"Any man of even subnormal intelligence," he remarked, "would have had sense enough to stay in the hospital until his physician was prepared to release him. Any mongoloid idiot would have known better than to go prancing around in your condition. It's a wonder to me those well-meant efforts at resuscitation didn't send a broken rib into a lung."

"I didn't," Hall said mildly, "set fire to my own house and, on the whole, I'd prefer a punctured lung to being a charred body."

The doctor grinned at him. "You'll live." At the door he turned back. "Unless you get involved in any more mayhem. Don't get up today."

Hall waited until he heard the doctor answering Mrs. Halsted's anxious inquiries and then went into the bathroom to take a shower. The cuts on his face, he noticed, while he shaved carefully around them, were healing nicely. The bruises, however, looked worse than ever, having acquired a spectacular range of color.

When he came out of the bathroom he found Halsted waiting for him. On the bed were packages and a suitbox.

"Underwear, socks, shoes, shirt, tie, and suit. I remembered that you and Robin wore the same size in everything."

"That was very kind."

"Oh, I cashed a check for you. A hundred dollars. Something to run on. Naturally you can draw on me for whatever you need until you get your own finances straightened out."

Halsted dismissed Hall's thanks with a vague gesture and watched him dress, noticing the stiffness of his movements, his difficulty in coping with socks and shoes.

"Did the doctor approve of your getting up?"

"It won't surprise him."

"You're a tough man to stop, Hall. That fire last night —"

"You say you didn't know anything about it until it was practically out?"

"Well, the couple is off for a week. The cook had been feeling the heat so Harriet packed the two of them off to Nantucket. They've been with us a long time. The gardeners don't live here. What with air-conditioning and our rooms being on the opposite side of the house we didn't hear a thing. If Harriet hadn't had a nightmare and waked up —"

"A nightmare?"

"Something on her mind, Hall. She isn't sleeping well. I'm worried about her. Since Lillian died she hasn't been like herself."

"Mr. Halsted, what did you and Lillian

quarrel about the morning of the day she died?"

There was a gasp from the doorway and Harriet Halsted plunged into the room. "That's nonsense, Hall! Bruce and Lillian never had a disagreement in their lives."

"Mrs. Williams overheard the quarrel," Hall told her. "She heard Lillian scream, 'You'll be sorry.' "

"You're going too far, prying into matters that don't concern you."

"Anything that has any bearing on those two deaths concerns me, Mrs. Halsted."

She looked into the unyielding face, so disturbingly like Robin's, so disturbingly unlike his. If only Hall would go away and stay away. If only he had never returned at all!

"And even suppose Bruce and Lillian had a little argument, what difference would that make?"

Halsted sighed. "You might as well try to talk a river into changing its course, Harriet. Save your breath. Hall won't be satisfied until he has raked up the whole thing. Let's go down to the bookroom where there's room for all of us to sit in comfort."

He stumped down the stairs, followed by his wife, with Hall bringing up the rear. He held hard to the railing. The combination of unaccustomed sleeping pills, suffocation, shock, and whatever dope the doctor had administered by hypodermic had left a residue of dizziness and uncertainty along with a curious heaviness about his movements.

Halsted tapped his fingers on the big desk. "I don't know how much Robin told you. I didn't want Lillian to marry him. The war had changed him. He was — I don't know how to describe it. Nothing concrete. But I know men. For months he had been in the thick of the fighting. You probably know his war record as well as I do. But he — used himself up. Physically, of course, he'd taken a lot of punishment, but it went deeper than that. I noticed it in little things. He couldn't settle down. He couldn't decide what to do with himself. He had become — indeterminate.

"Lillian lost her head over him and I could understand that. He had good looks, the glamour of his war record, exceptional charm — he never lost that. But he was — empty, Hall.

"Well," he went on heavily, "Lillian got her own way, of course, and they were married. After that I never said a word. Not a word. Even when Robin got tied up with that scoundrel Welford. Not that he discussed it with me. He knew my views.

"Well, the day — they died, Lillian called

157

early in the morning. She was hysterical. She said someone had been blackmailing Robin, that he had paid out thirty thousand dollars. He'd just had a letter demanding a final payment of forty thousand by July the fourth. And he couldn't raise it. Would I help? I told her to come over here and tried to get the story out of her."

"What did the blackmailer have on Robin?"

"I don't know."

"Who was it?"

Halsted raised his hands from the desk, dropped them. "I don't know. But Lillian wanted me to put up the money." After a pause he said, "For Robin's sake, of course. Naturally I refused."

"And later that day," Hall said, "she told an unknown man that she would pay his debt. I wonder whether she did. Has any examination been made of her personal banking account?"

"Lillian didn't have forty thousand. Probably not more than three or four."

"Are you sure, Mr. Halsted, that it was Robin who was being blackmailed and not Lillian?"

Halsted's face was mottled with fury. "You — you," he mouthed, "get out of here."

"Bruce!" his wife cried in alarm.

"Get out!"

Without a word Hall walked out of the room, out of the house.

II

For a few minutes he went back to survey the burned-out shell of the Cape Cod cottage. Whatever had happened there, no trace remained now. And no trace, he remembered with a surge of relief, of Robin's note to Welford.

Then he turned back and passed the Halsted house without a glance. It occurred to him that he had no roof over his head and no place to go. Perhaps he should find out who handled the insurance and report the fire, but Halsted was the only one who could tell him and at this point he was unlikely to tell him anything.

"Well," a cheerful voice said, "I didn't expect to see you up so soon, Mr. Masson. Have you been surveying the damage?"

"Mrs. Williams, isn't it?"

"Yes, and such a lot of excitement you've let me in for!"

"I have?" he said in surprise.

"Well, the fire really. And, by the way, my husband's agency handles the insurance, you know."

"That's helpful. I didn't know whom to ask."

"He's at the office now, of course, but do come in. I have something exciting to tell you. In fact, I was just going to tidy up a bit before I went to the police. Of course, I could call them but I've never seen the inside of a State Police Barracks and this is my one great adventure. I don't want to miss a minute of it."

Hall followed the chattering woman into the big barn-like house. This, too, was modern but in a different style from Welford's. An imaginative architect had designed it to fit into the wooded land on which it stood so that the outdoors had been brought artfully inside.

He looked around him with pleasure. "This is delightful!"

"What can I bring you? Some tea or a drink or — have you lunched?"

"I had a late breakfast."

"Then just a cup of homemade soup and maybe a small sandwich."

While she bustled around her kitchen Hall looked out of the window. The red mailbox at the end of the drive was as visible from here as the obelisk. He saw the street lamp directly over it. To whom, he wondered, had Lillian mailed a letter a few minutes before her death?

"Well," Mrs. Williams said eagerly when she had set a tray before him, "just a bite but it's a real nourishing soup and you ought to keep up your strength."

He laughed and was surprised to find that he was really hungry.

"The thing is," Mrs. Williams began, "that I had a feeling I had seen that boy before, the one who set fire to your house. Just a vague impression, you know, but it was like a name you can't remember. Stop thinking of it and it comes to you. In a blinding flash. And that's exactly what happened. More soup? There's a whole kettleful."

"Thank you, no. That was delicious and I am most appreciative."

"So this morning I said to Mr. Williams, 'I know I've seen that boy before,' and he said they all try to look alike now. But anyhow just as he was going to work he said he'd better stop for some gas because the tank of his station wagon was registering practically empty. And of course in his business — well, anyhow, I knew right then and there that I'd seen that boy at a garage somewhere.

"Well, all the time I was making beds and straightening up it kept nagging at me. So the long and short of it is that after lunch — I couldn't start before then because I'd promised to bake some cookies for the church fair — I just got in my little Ford and started out. I went to every garage in the village and on the outskirts, though why they need so many

I'm sure I don't know. So I was getting dis-
couraged. I knew what Mr. Williams would
say."

She waited expectantly so Hall obliged.
"What would he say?"

"He'd say, like he always does, 'You get
the craziest ideas, honey.' But still — well,
after all, you know how it is. You stop for
gas when you need it and not necessarily in
the village. So I went on, broadened the
search, you might say, as far as Brookview.
I couldn't remember that we had ever bought
gas there but still — anyhow, I pulled up at
the pump and a fellow I'd never seen before
came out to fill the tank. I was just about
to give up when I looked inside the place
where they repair cars, you know what I
mean, and there was the very boy!"

"You're sure about that, Mrs. Williams?"

"I'd swear to it on a stack of Bibles."

"You might have to, you know."

Mrs. Williams glowed. "I can hardly wait."

With some reluctance she gave Hall
the name of the garage and described the
boy. With greater reluctance she promised
to hold herself at Captain Gerfind's disposal
but to do nothing until he got in touch with
her.

Seeing her disappointment Hall said,
"You've been invaluable, Mrs. Williams." He

added impressively, "You may have broken the case."

Having made her completely happy he took his leave. On the sidewalk above the Green he paused to decide where he would go next. A car door slammed and he saw the Buick convertible move away from the Halsted house. Gail caught sight of him and pulled in at the curb. This time he managed to open the door himself but he found it difficult to close. Gail had to lean across him to reach it. As she straightened up, flushing, he put his hand on hers.

"What's wrong?"

"Wrong!" she said furiously. "I go to your house and it's been burned practically to the ground and no sign of you and the Halsteds wouldn't say anything except you weren't there, even if you were all right, even if you were alive. And — damn it, I'm not crying! I don't care what happens to you. A — a bumbling idiot who gets himself slashed and kicked and burned —"

She put her head on her folded arms on the wheel and wailed aloud.

ELEVEN

"Darling," Hall said at last, "we've simply got to move on. We're beginning to attract an audience."

Gail sat up abruptly, blew her nose, and started the car.

"Do you mind our going to your house? I haven't any place of my own now where we can talk. And I think we'll have to talk."

Gail sniffled. "There's nothing to talk about."

"Your house. Please, Gail."

Once more Gail turned into the narrow driveway. She admitted him to the Carlyle half of the duplex, and when she had closed the door she faced him defiantly.

He pulled her into his arms, turned her face toward him, kissed her until she pushed him back, flushed and breathless.

"Hall, I told you —"

"That it is impossible. Is it, Gail?" He pulled her close to him with a kind of violence. "I love you. And you know it." When she made no response he gave her a little shake. "Don't you?"

"You've probably torn loose that strapping," she said crossly.

"I wouldn't be surprised." He was laughing at her. "Come back here."

She was retreating toward the living room. "You're very confident, aren't you? Very sure of me. Because — I was upset. So you took for granted —"

"Not sure, no." He made no attempt to follow her. If only his head weren't so dizzy, his feet so leaden, his body still half doped. He moved as casually as he could to lean against the hall table for support. "I've fallen in love with you, as you know perfectly well. You tell me it's impossible. Your brother came last night to tell me it's impossible. But it has happened. I hoped it had happened to you, too."

She was watching him now, her wide brown eyes intent. "Last night? Greg came to see you last night? Why?"

"To warn me to stay away from you. I told him I loved you and he said, as you do, that it's impossible."

"Last night."

"Oh." He began to laugh. "In case you have any more peculiar ideas — and you seem to harbor a great many peculiar ideas, my darling — your brother did not set fire to my house. Mrs. Williams saw the boy who did it."

She expelled a long breath. "I never for a moment," she said unconvincingly, "suspected Greg of anything so ridiculous."

"Why should you?" When she made no reply he said gently, "It's a simple question, you know. A quite reasonable question." For a moment a wave of blackness surged over his eyes, his head.

"You look terribly white!" she exclaimed. "For heaven's sake, sit down."

He held more firmly to the table until his eyes cleared. "Time is running out on me. In less than two weeks I have to get back to my own job."

"But what can you do now? Please, Hall, don't be a fool!"

"At this point," he agreed, "I'm not much of a man, God knows, but I'm not so decrepit that I'll answer for the consequences if we stay here together any longer. Are you still driving for me?"

She caught up the car keys and brushed past him hastily, aware of his eyes watching the color rise in her face.

"Where now?" she asked when she was safely behind the wheel of the Buick.

"Brookview."

She looked at him in surprise. "Why on earth —"

"Because at a garage in Brookview I think we'll find the boy who set fire to my house."

When he had reported Mrs. Williams's

story she asked, "Do you think she is reliable?"

"Absolutely, I should say. Not enough imagination to invent things. An accurate observer. She'll be a good witness on the stand, too, if things ever get that far. She's so patently honest that her testimony would carry a lot of weight."

"But, Hall, why do you think the boy did it?"

"I assume he was simply carrying out Welford's orders."

"You mean Welford found out that I took the stuff from his files?"

"I took it." Hall's tone was unexpectedly forceful. "Remember that, Gail. You had nothing to do with the business. Nothing whatever. The responsibility is mine. I want you to get that straight. Is it clear?"

"Perfectly clear," she said sweetly. "I simply love masterful men."

"Sorry. I didn't mean to order you about."

"Somehow I thought that was exactly what you meant."

He laughed. "You are an infuriating woman, my beloved, but I do wish you were more of a yielding type. And more — susceptible, shall I say?"

She ignored the mischief in his face. "Hall," she said quietly, her hands tightening on the wheel, "there's a car following us. I've noticed it ever since we left the house. That's why I've been taking those side roads. I wanted to see whether we'd lose it."

He tried to turn in the seat, abandoned the effort. "Are you sure?"

She nodded. "Never mind. Here's Brookview. If the car follows us to the garage I'll call the police or scream bloody murder. You can't take much more assault and battery."

"For once in my life I'd like to prove myself a man of action. Instead, just when I want to make a good impression on my girl I seem to have developed the habit of letting her protect me."

She pulled up at the pumps. Hall looked with interest at the boy who had come out of the garage.

"Hello, Jake," Gail said in surprise and recognition, "when did you start working here?"

Hall leaned forward. "Harry sent him down; I heard him say so." He looked the boy over and was aware that he was the young punk he had noticed the day he reached Shelton. "After that attack on me." He pushed open the door with a grunt and climbed out. "Do you still carry a knife, Jake?"

The boy had come around the car and was edging toward him, his hand in his pocket, tossing the long hair out of his eyes. From inside the garage another boy was moving in their direction, a boy with a discolored lump on his chin. The two were closing in, forcing Hall back against the car.

A horn blared in the car that had drawn up behind the Buick, both doors opened; Captain Gerfind and a trooper reached them in long strides. The trooper seized Jake's arm, struck the knife out of his hand, snapped handcuffs on the snarling boy.

The other boy began to run. Captain Gerfind shouted an order. The boy called a mocking phrase, ran on. Gerfind fired one shot over his head and the boy jolted to a halt, came back slowly, showing the whites of his eyes like a frightened horse.

"Who are you?"

"Max Brenner," the boy said sullenly.

"And you?"

"Jake Collins."

"Whose garage is this?"

"Harry Wilkes owns it but he's trying to sell."

Gerfind looked at Hall. "Why," he asked plaintively, but more in anger than in sorrow, "can't you leave this to us? I had a hunch you'd get yourself in more trouble."

"Is that why you were following us?"

Gerfind grinned. "That and curiosity. What were you looking for this time?"

"The boy who set fire to my house. Mrs. Williams saw him here this morning, and I'd heard Harry say he sent Jake down yesterday, so Max must be the one I want."

"You seem to have a gift for turning over stones. This time," and the captain stopped grinning, "I prefer to pick up what's underneath, myself." He turned to Max. "Who ordered you to set fire to the Masson house?"

Max's weak mouth curled in a sneer. "No one gives me orders, Copper."

Gerfind winked broadly at Hall. "Pitiful, isn't it? These young punks will believe anything they are told if they are flattered enough. Told they're as smart as anyone. Told a guy with a knife is better than a guy without a knife. Told it's clever to burn down houses though they haven't the brains to build one. Told they are protecting the country though they don't know what the country stands for. Bait! That's all they are. Bait to catch fish.

"Funny thing," he went on, his savage tone gone, his manner almost genial, still addressing Hall, ignoring the boy's impotent fury, "they just don't know it's always scum these pint-size Hitlers make use of."

"You —" The boy spat forth a flood of obscenity and Gerfind shoved a hand over his mouth. He nodded to the trooper. "We're taking them in. Booking them."

170

"What for?" Max asked when Gerfind had removed his hand. The belligerence was gone. He was cringing.

"Jake here on assault and battery with intent to kill."

"Kill!" Jake howled. "We was just going to rough him up, teach him to keep his nose out of our business."

"Shut up," Max warned him.

"And you," Gerfind said to Max, "on the same charge. Plus arson. Purdy, call Mrs. Williams and we'll pin down that identification."

The trooper nodded and steered the boys, handcuffed together, into the back seat of the unmarked police car. Then the captain slid under the wheel.

"Do go home and leave this to us, Mr. Masson. You are beginning to take up too much of my time."

"I'd like to ask one question," Hall said.

"Only one," the captain warned him.

"Who gave Max his orders and showed him how to make an incendiary bomb?"

The trooper made a slight gesture and Max cringed. He'd been brought up in a neighborhood that regards the police as its natural enemy.

"It was Mr. Welford, and I can tell you dopes one thing for sure. He won't stand for this."

"You alarm me," Gerfind said gravely and he started the car.

II

"There is a certain stimulation about your company, Mr. Masson," Gail remarked when they had pulled away from the garage, "but it is hardly restful."

"I'm not sure I want you to find me restful," Hall admitted, "but I'm past apologizing for getting you involved in nasty situations."

"What can you expect with the company you keep?"

"Not very choice specimens," he agreed. "In the future I'll try to do better. Much better. It could be a nice future, Gail."

"And what do you plan for the immediate future?"

"Such a lovely voice and such a discouraging attitude."

"I wish you'd be serious for once."

"I am. Deadly serious." There was no laughter in his voice now.

"What nefarious deed are you planning?"

"At the moment I am going to appeal to Mr. Burgess and see whether he'll take me in for the night. Until I can handle the car myself I'd like to stay in Shelton. There should be some extra beds in that old place of his, wouldn't you think?"

"I suppose so, though I doubt if he uses more than the ground floor. He has lived alone there for twenty years, I understand, since his wife died and his married daughter moved to the Middle West somewhere. There's a cleaning woman who comes in twice a week and he gets his own meals."

"How on earth did you find out all this?" Hall asked curiously.

"Well, he's lonely, the poor old man, and his office is in the library, so we talk now and then."

As usual, Burgess sat at his desk in the basement of the library, but today there was no teen-ager as captive audience. The old man was deep in thought and there seemed to be new lines etched in his face. He got to his feet and pulled out a chair for Gail while Hall perched on the edge of the desk.

"No young men today?" Hall asked.

"I've been made a fool of," Burgess said. "Welford made a fool of me. I wanted those boys given another chance and Welford has made unscrupulous, criminal use of them."

"I don't see how you can blame yourself, Mr. Burgess," Gail said warmly. "You were doing your very best."

"But knowing what Welford was, I should have guessed that he had some trick up his sleeve. I didn't realize he could still be dangerous —" Burgess broke off, looked at Hall in embarrassment.

The latter put his hand on the teacher's shoulder. "It's all right. I know about Robin's part in Welford's campaign. He was caught in a kind of trap but he was through; he wouldn't have gone on with it."

Burgess gave him an odd look. "You may be right. In any case —"

"In any case," Hall said briskly, "we know now that Welford incited that attack on me and the burning of my house. By the time Captain Gerfind has checked out the fingerprints on the typewriter and traced that incendiary bomb back to him, Welford will have his teeth drawn."

The old man brightened. "I pray so. I pray so. If I could only have some part —"

"What you could do, if you would be so kind, would be to put me up for a couple of nights."

Burgess beamed. "Delighted. Mrs. Benham is at the house now. I'll call and ask her to make up a bed for you. Actually, it's only a couch in my study, but most comfortable. I shut off the upper floors years ago. The oil bill — dreadful what it costs to live these days."

"I won't inconvenience you too much?"

"You would give me the greatest pleasure. Someone to talk to in the evenings. I'm a bit of a night owl, you know, and sometimes the nights seem very long."

That night did not seem long to Hall. Burgess's couch in the small, overcrowded room he called his study was made of down, wide and deep and soft, and the linen sheets were faintly scented with old-fashioned lavender. Even discomfort would not have kept him awake and he slept for ten hours.

He awakened with a feeling of well-being he had not experienced since he had received the news of his brother's death and he faced his delighted host at the breakfast table able to announce that he was fully recovered, or that he would be as soon as the doctor removed the strapping.

"Just the same, you must take care of yourself," Burgess insisted. "I understand from Captain Gerfind —"

"You've talked to him?"

"He called last night but I refused to waken you. Anyone who could sleep through that ringing needed his sleep."

Hall pushed back his chair. "I'd better call him."

"He'll get in touch with you later. He said he'd be away from the barracks most of the morning. He has pulled in all the boys on that list for questioning. My boys." Burgess's purplish lips twitched wryly. "Welford's boys. There seems to be no question now that Welford was engineering their activities."

"What does Gerfind intend to do about our local fascist?"

"I don't know. I got the impression that Captain Gerfind is off on another tack entirely."

"How did he know where to find me?"

"He called Miss Carlyle. I understand her brother said first that she knew nothing about you. There seems to have been a bit of an argument."

"Oh, lord! I've made almost every mistake a man could make where she is concerned."

Burgess smiled. "That wasn't my impression." He refilled Hall's coffee cup.

"Mr. Burgess, what did you mean when you said that the fact my aunt had disinherited me might be the answer to Lillian's death? And, by the way, did you receive a letter from Lillian the day after she died?"

"A letter from Mrs. Masson!" The old man was astonished. "No. She never wrote to me at any time." He pressed his hands together. His face was profoundly sad. "When I said that about your disinheritance it was really Robin I was thinking of. What with your various mishaps and Welford's disgusting activities, I think we've rather lost sight of Robin."

"I haven't," Hall assured him grimly.

"You see, I knew you both so well. I knew how grave an injustice your aunt had done you, had done both of you, perhaps. I've always felt that too much indulgence helps to destroy character."

He held up his hand as Hall started to speak. "When I learned that your aunt had disinherited you and sent you away I was most indignant. You never told her, did you, why you needed that fifteen thousand? She believed it was to cover some peccadillo of your own. But I knew you both and when Robin didn't finish his first year at college, when he never went back, I investigated. At that time I still had some faculty friends. All dead now. Every man of them. Well, I found out what had happened. Robin had a fight with Welford, who lost an eye as a result. You paid Welford fifteen thousand dollars as compensation."

"I saw that fight. Welford began it. What happened to him was sheer accident. Robin was sick about it."

"But he let you take the blame."

"That," Hall said, "was entirely my own idea. My aunt idolized him. She'd have been horribly hurt and upset. This made it easier for her."

"And for Robin." The gentle voice was relentless.

"But what the long-forgotten episode has to do with Lillian's death I can't imagine."

"Robin needed admiration, Hall. He had had it all his life. Now, with that obelisk to live up to, he was vulnerable. Very vulnerable. He fell into Welford's hands and let himself be used in order to protect his public image. But I feel convinced that Lillian turned against him in disillusionment."

"What are you trying to say?" Hall's voice was strained.

"I think Robin shot her, Hall. If you stick to plain facts there is no one else on God's green earth who had any reason to kill her."

TWELVE

The official voice was not authorized to give out information about the boys who had been brought in for questioning. He could not say whether any more evidence had turned up on the Masson murder case. Captain Gerfind had not returned to the barracks.

Hall dialed the Carlyle number and waited while the telephone rang nine times.

Apparently he was going to spend a frustrating morning and he had only twelve days left in which to get at the truth behind the deaths of Robin and Lillian.

At length he called Mrs. Williams and asked for the name of her husband's insurance agency. She greeted him with a little cry of delight. She had gone to the State Police Barracks where she had identified Max Brenner as the boy who had hurled the incendiary bomb at the roof of the Masson house. They had asked her to pick him out of a group of a dozen boys.

"All so mangy-looking," she exclaimed, "and Mr. Williams is anxious to discuss the matter with you. The Shelton agency. He sent for his own investigator to try to find where that incendiary bomb came from. And, my dear, it seems to have been made right here in Shelton, and the boys — I can hardly believe it — say it was Millard Welford's idea. Such a good-looking man and always so close to your brother. He was just leaving the police barracks with his lawyer when I got there and he looked like a thundercloud. Such a pleasant manner he always seemed to have. Aren't people —"

Hall waited patiently for her to run down. A car came to a screaming halt and he excused himself hastily. Gail at last. Then the front door crashed back against the wall as though someone were trying to tear it off its hinges.

"Welford!"

"I've come to give you fair warning. You take me off the hook with the police or I'll have you and Gail Carlyle arrested for breaking and entering and theft. I'll drag that girl through so much mud she'll never be able to scrape it off."

"You so much as whisper her name, Welford, and you'll never know what hit you."

Hall braced himself to meet that onward rush. He ducked as Welford's fist lashed at his jaw. Then Welford smashed at his face, lost his balance as a small rug slipped on the waxed floor, and went down with a crash.

Hall hurled himself on the other man. There

was a rush of blood up the back of his neck and head. He saw Welford through a red glaze. His hands closed on his throat, slipped on the collar, tightened slowly. He was dimly aware that Welford was clawing at his hands, smashing his defenseless face, straining to throw him off, but he held on. He was going to kill Welford.

The other man was in better condition and he was angry, but Hall was a killer. Nothing could have shaken him off, nothing could have loosened his hold. Through that red glaze he saw the knowledge growing in Welford's face, knew that his struggle was diminishing, saw the horror in the reddened eyes.

And suddenly sanity returned. Hall released his hold, got to his feet, found a chair and dropped into it weakly. The madness was over. He was completely spent. The outcome of the fight seemed no longer to matter.

Welford drew in gasping breaths and pulled himself up.

"For God's sake," he said at last. "For God's sake! You were going to kill me."

"What did you expect? I've got a big score to settle with you, Welford. But not that way. That's your way. You and your kind. I'm going to leave you to the law."

"Why are you trying to wreck me, Masson? That's what it amounts to. What are you trying to accomplish?" Welford sounded bewildered.

"Why were my brother and his wife killed?"

"I don't know. I swear to God I don't know. They were alive and well when Freda and I left that night. And I had no motive. Robin was worth his weight in gold to me."

"But Robin had refused to go on backing you."

"He changed his mind that night."

Hall did not attempt to reply. He simply shook his head.

"But to kill him for that! For God's sake, Masson, use your head."

"What's this sudden reaction against killing? You set your goons on me with knives, three to one. If Carlyle hadn't come along they'd have finished me off. You sent one of them to burn down my house because you thought the evidence against you was still there. If it hadn't been for Harry Wilkes I'd have burned to death. Are you seriously trying to convince me that you balk at killing?"

"A bunch of kids," Welford said. "Irresponsible. You can't pin the responsibility for their actions on me."

"I can try. What's more, they'll help, simply to clear themselves."

"You just don't understand," Welford said. "A confused liberal like you can't understand.

People have to be led. Damn it, they want to be led. They like being told what to do, what to think."

"And who," Hall asked, "tells you what to do, what to think?"

"I can't reach you," Welford complained. "You are blinded by prejudice."

Hall made an impatient gesture. "Cut out the dialectics. You're not equipped. And you never sold Robin on your ideas either. What was your hold on him?"

Unexpectedly Welford laughed. Then he saw Hall's expression. "I don't know. That's what is so funny."

"I don't see the joke yet."

"One night I stopped in for a quick one at a tavern in Brookview. Harry Wilkes was there. He'd had a couple before I came in. We had a couple more. I said a few words about the new party, about getting enough names on that petition so we could make a good showing. What I needed was an approach to someone like Bruce Halsted because he has the kind of community prestige that's so useful. But Halsted's hidebound; he wouldn't give me the time of day. And Harry said why not try Lieutenant Masson, if it was prestige I wanted. War hero. Married to the Halsted girl. Maybe get two birds with one stone."

Welford lighted a cigarette, trying to steady

183

the match. He had difficulty in making contact. He had just grazed death and he knew it.

"Well?"

Welford looked uneasily at Hall Masson. He had never suspected the killer latent in him. Just a professor-type man, he had thought.

"Well, we'd had that fight in college and we weren't exactly buddy-buddy. I didn't see any approach there, though I knew his support could make all the difference. So Harry asked if I knew the lieutenant's wife and I said we didn't move in the same circles. And he said the lieutenant was nuts about her. So we talked of this and that. Harry was stoned by that time. Well, I was leaving when he said, 'If you want the lieutenant's support just mention Gregory Carlyle to him. Drop the name and watch the reaction. It might do the trick.' And he passed out. I got him home and I don't suppose he's remembered it since. But I —"

"You mentioned Gregory Carlyle to Robin."

"Just in passing. Said he was a nice fellow. Said Robin knew him, of course. I was groping in the dark because I didn't know the score — unless Lillian Masson and Carlyle were having fun and games. But — well, Robin sat there, looking queer, and then he said he'd back me as far as he could."

"But when he refused to support you he and Lillian died."

"I didn't kill them. I don't know who killed them. And I'll tell you this, Masson, the reason I tried to get you out of town was because I didn't want this business of the murders raked up."

"I believe you."

"Not because I had any part in them but because I wanted your brother's name and prestige behind me. I wanted him — still heroic. And I knew that what was raked up would destroy the value of his backing. He was hiding something, though God knows what it was. My own hunch is that his wife was messed up with Carlyle — he's a widower, you know — and Robin was trying to protect her. She was in a state that last night at dinner. She had been crying. Freda said she acted kind of feverish. The two girls sat on the lawn while Robin and I talked business in his study upstairs."

"What really happened up there?"

"He just sat staring at me, kind of dulled. He didn't pay much attention. I don't think he even heard what I was saying. At last he got up and said, 'What's the use, Millard? We're all washed up. Everything is all washed up. Now clear out, will you?' And that's the last time I saw him."

Welford pulled his collar straight, used a pocket comb on his hair, looked from Masson to the disordered room.

"A couple of buffaloes might have been let loose. Poor old Burgess! Want me to help you straighten up?"

Together the two men restored order to Burgess's cluttered living room and then Welford said, "Look here, Masson, I'll make a bargain with you."

Hall's eyebrows arched. "Will you, indeed?"

"Get me off the hook with the police and I'll keep Gail Carlyle's name out."

"This," Hall reminded him, "is where you came in."

"I can explain about the kids. And as long as the rest of the stuff was burned up —"

"Your mistake," Hall said. "I got rid of that before the fire. The list of boys and the set of instructions for inciting to violence are in the hands of the police. We're going to see that that story hits the press and the radio and television. You're all through, Welford."

II

Burgess did not return for lunch. He had gone to the police barracks where, perhaps, he could put in a word for his boys.

186

Hall foraged for himself, made a corn beef sandwich, and opened a bottle of beer. Eating and drinking proved to be painful because of his split and bruised mouth. His scrap with Welford hadn't done him any good and his face was swollen and puffy from the blows that had been hammered at it.

He sprawled in an easy chair in Burgess's living room, too weary to move. With the ebbing of his murderous rage he was emotionally spent. The path he had been following was marked "Dead end." Welford had not killed Robin and Lillian. He had not been the blackmailer. Oddly enough, Hall had believed him when he said that he had wanted to save Robin's reputation. And once more Hall found himself wondering futilely what had happened during the three hours that followed Lillian's death.

Lillian and Gregory Carlyle? According to Mrs. Cushing, Robin had taken to watching his wife. So, after all, it might be on Lillian's account that he had paid blackmail.

Up to a point Welford had told the truth. Whatever hold he had on Robin he had acquired as a result of Harry's hints, and Harry had a brand-new garage.

Hall called the State Police Barracks once more. Captain Gerfind was at lunch. Yes, he would be told that Mr. Masson wanted to reach him as soon as possible.

The bell rang and Hall went to the door.

Gail looked at him in consternation. "Now what have you done to yourself?"

"Had a little argument with Welford."

"You are practically out on your feet. Sit down — no, over there where I'll have more light. Good heavens, that cut over your eye is bleeding and so is your mouth and — dear heaven, did he try to kill you?"

"I think," Hall said carefully, "that I tried to kill him. It's rather a traumatic experience, discovering what you're capable of doing."

"Why in heaven's name did you try to kill him?"

Hall found it impossible to say that he had, literally, seen red when Welford threatened to drag her through the mud. She wasn't the kind of girl to relish so primitive an action. It took the wholly womanly woman to enjoy having a couple of males battling over her.

"Tit for tat," he said lightly. "I rob his files. He burns down my house to destroy them. I call the attention of the police to his activities. He decides to rough me up. I — discover I've got it in me to kill a man in cold blood."

"But you didn't."

"By the grace of God. Don't go away."

"I'm just going to get some hot water and

some bandages if there are any. That is, if you can sit quietly and not get into any more trouble until I come back."

She worked on his battered face with gentle, competent hands, and then sat back on her heels beside his chair, regarding him doubtfully.

"That's the best I can do but I must say you look thoroughly disreputable."

He put out a hand as she started to get up. "Why didn't you come this morning? Where were you?"

"Greg took the keys to the Buick so I couldn't drive for you. I had to walk to the plant — he's manager of that electronics outfit — three miles out of town." She laughed up at him. "He was in conference so I barged in and asked for the keys. He couldn't risk a scene so —" She dangled the keys triumphantly in her hand. "But I might have known. Leave you alone for a morning and you get into trouble. I suppose you wouldn't consider following Captain Gerfind's advice and leaving this to the police."

"I doubt if Welford would have confided in them to the same extent."

"You've learned something!" There was alarm in the quick look she gave him.

"Someone was blackmailing my brother. He had paid out thirty thousand dollars. A final

189

payment of forty thousand was demanded the morning of the day he died. I think Harry Wilkes was blackmailing him and that Robin couldn't raise the final payment so he killed him."

"But blackmailers don't kill!"

"Harry needed that money to establish himself as respectable and important in the community. It's a driving passion with him."

"But it's a ridiculous reason for murder."

"Of course. But there's no adequate reason for murder. I discovered that this morning." The telephone rang and Hall got up to answer it.

"Hear you've been calling me," Captain Gerfind said.

"I have some news for you and I want some information."

"What now?" It occurred to Hall that Gerfind seemed to be in high good humor.

"Could you find out where Harry Wilkes raised the money for his new service station?"

"I'll be damned! You must have a crystal ball. Just checked things out at the Brookview bank this morning. My brother-in-law works there. Harry Wilkes has a safety deposit box and he's been making deposits in his checking account in cash, small bills. Started right after the lieutenant began to make his withdrawals

190

from the Shelton bank. The old garage in Brookview was bankrupt. The new one was built for cash."

"So we've got us a blackmailer," Hall said in a tone of satisfaction.

"Looks like it. I'm pulling Wilkes in for a little talk as soon as I've finished checking out these boys. The queer thing is that while the boys who roughed you up and wrote the anonymous letter — those were Jake's prints on the typewriter — and set fire to the house were Harry's employees, they deny that he had anything to do with their outside activities. They are falling over themselves to lay the blame on Welford. I think they've been a bit afraid of him all along; too rich for their blood. Now they know he doesn't carry guaranteed immunity with him they want out. They say Harry hired them to give them a chance. He is strict but fair. He gives them time out for their interviews with Burgess. He gave them fair warning that if they got into trouble they would be fired. He wants his business run straight."

Hall laughed suddenly. "On blackmail money."

"There are bigger businesses based on worse than that."

"I believe you. Well, thanks a lot."

"I'll be in touch. You — keep — out." The

words were spaced for emphasis.

When Hall returned he found Gail pulling on white gloves.

"You," he told her firmly, "are going home. I've involved you enough. Your brother is quite right."

"Where are you going?"

"To Harry's Service Station. And I don't need the car for that."

"Still," she pointed out, "it will look more natural, won't it, for us to drive up for gas."

"Us?"

She picked up the keys and went out to start the car. "If you walk, I'll follow you, playing a fanfare on the horn all the way."

"I believe you would."

There was a new boy at the pumps and while he filled the tank Hall got out and strolled toward the office. Gail went after him. The little office was empty and then Harry came in from the garage.

"Oh, God, not you again!" He did a double take. "Your face looks like raw beef. Wish I could have seen it."

"Well, you can't have everything."

"Keep out of my way, Masson. I've had the police around here and they've taken two of my best boys and the work is getting behind."

"Tough," Hall sympathized.

"Look here, I've got the picture. Welford has been using some of these kids as troublemakers. But I didn't know anything about it and you can't prove I did. All I've done was to send a couple of them over to the old place at Brookview, trying to straighten them out. They're not bad kids, just mugs who didn't know better. Why I just got put on the church committee for better citizenship. I can't afford this sort of thing. I'm no floater. I want to live here the rest of my life, and live respected. Now get lost!"

Hall leaned against a display case. "What was in the letter my sister-in-law wrote you?"

Harry's astonishment seemed to be real. "She never wrote me a letter in her life."

"You didn't know her?"

"Not to speak to."

"You were seen having lunch with her at the Stagecoach the day she died."

Harry chuckled. "You sure scatter your shot, hoping you'll hit something. No, Mister Wise Guy, I did not have lunch at the Stagecoach or any other place with Mrs. Masson. She'd lived here all her life but she didn't even remember my face. And for that day I have a swell alibi. I took time off at noon to give blood at the hospital. I do it regular."

He leaned forward, his big fists clenched.

"Get off my back, Masson! No one tears down this position I'm building."

"Building with my brother's money. Thirty thousand dollars. Nice going, Harry, but blackmail's a prison offense."

At something in the garage man's face, Hall shifted his position so that he stood in front of Gail.

"So you think maybe you can prove it," Harry said at last. "You can break me. Okay, go ahead. All I've worked for will be gone. My wife won't be able to hold up her head with her snooty family."

"You're breaking my heart."

"Yeah? Well, maybe I can at that. Say blackmail to anyone else and I'm going to see that obelisk gets a coat of yellow that will never come off."

Harry looked at Gail. "Ask her. Ask why she's been following you around, watching every move you make. And if she won't talk I will. Ask her why your brother paid off — and glad to. Glad to, mind. So I'd keep my mouth shut, keep that obelisk nice and clean, keep our hero out of prison.

"And why? Because he killed Gregory Carlyle's wife, that's why. Hit-run. The yellow-livered coward! Our hero! Yah! And then the damned fool brought his car to me for repairs."

194

There was a long silence in the office. "So if you're wondering who killed the lieutenant and his wife, ask Gregory Carlyle."

THIRTEEN

Gail had pulled the car off the road in the shade of maples that lined the river. Rocks showed above the shallow water that danced and sparkled in the sunlight. A light breeze stirred the leaves. Gail sat staring straight ahead of her. Neither of them had spoken since they left Harry's Service Station.

When Hall spoke at last it was not to ask a question. "You knew. That's why you tried to drive me away that first night; why you've been so — helpful."

She winced as though he had struck her but she answered calmly enough, "That's why."

For a moment he occupied himself in filling and lighting his pipe. "Just what did you hope to accomplish?" There was only detached interest in his voice.

"I don't know."

"Oh, come now. There's no more need for skirmishing. Let's try being honest for a change. It's not so difficult once you get the hang of it."

"If you are going to be offensive —" She reached for the keys but Hall, with a quick gesture, forestalled her, pulled them out, and dropped them in his pocket.

"We're going to talk," he reminded her when the silence had lasted a long time, "and this time we're going to have all the facts."

"I told you once before you wouldn't like what you found."

"That doesn't really matter, does it?"

She looked at him, incredulity in her face. "You don't care?"

"Of course I care, but that's not the point. People can't live by illusion alone, by dodging the issues, by pretending they aren't there."

Gail said unexpectedly, "You think people can't live entirely with illusion, but they can't live entirely without it. Call it what you will: dreams or aspirations or — heroes."

His eyes were intent on her face now. He had removed his glasses and she saw how light and cold his eyes were.

"Are you trying to help me keep a heroic picture of my brother?"

She flung out her hand. "Would it have done any harm?"

"The man you called a phony?"

"Oh, what's the use!"

"None at all. It wasn't my brother you were protecting, obviously; it was yours."

"Can you blame me for that? Greg and

Martha were so happy together and he's been — just lost without her. And bitter. Because a man ran her down and killed her and then ran away."

"How did it happen? Do you know?"

"She'd gone shopping. She wasn't supposed to carry heavy bundles but Greg had the car that day and so —"

"Why wasn't she?"

"Well, she'd been having dizzy spells. The doctor had been going over her, making tests, but he hadn't found out what was causing her trouble."

"So she could have fallen under the car. Robin might not have been able to stop in time."

"Well — I suppose so. In any case, he didn't stay there or report it."

"Would your brother's loss and grief have been lessened if he had stopped? Would Martha have been less dead?"

"Are you trying to defend your brother?"

"I'm trying to discover what his real crime was. Not to maintain that hero image. Don't misunderstand me. I've never believed in heroes. It's hard enough for a man to make a go at being a man without having to take on a hero's stature. It wasn't for his heroism I loved him. It was for the only reason that counts, because he was himself, good and bad all mixed up, strength and weakness, the lot.

"I think no one will deny that his war record was terrific. Over and beyond the call of duty. But there are limits to endurance just as there are to intelligence. What with all his physical injuries and a kind of spiritual exhaustion, he hadn't any reserves. If he ran away — well, who doesn't, now and then? I'm not condoning, Gail; I'm explaining."

"Then you think he shouldn't be punished?"

He turned toward her his astonished face. "God! Don't you think he was punished?"

"But it doesn't help Greg."

"Wasn't it you who said it was vengeance I was after? An eye for an eye. And all the time you knew that your brother had shot Robin and Lillian."

"No. Oh, no, no!" She looked at the key he had put in the switch. "What are you going to do?"

"I am going to ask your brother some pertinent questions."

"Hall —"

He shook his head. "Don't remind me that I'm in love with you. It won't do any good."

"You'd be a very easy man to hate."

"So a number of people have made clear in the past few days. Let's get going."

II

There was a shabby Ford in the driveway beside the duplex. Gail pulled up behind it, shut off the motor of the Buick and handed Hall the keys.

"I won't be using them again." She waited, tall and slim, her face and shoulders stiff with hostility, while he got out of the car. This time she made no effort to help him.

Gregory Carlyle, a highball in his hand, was sitting in the living room, looking at the evening paper.

"Damn it," he said without looking up, "you played a dirty trick on me with those keys. I told you to stay away from that guy."

"She was covering for you," Hall said and Greg upset his drink as he got out of his chair.

"No, Greg!" Gail cried as he started for Hall.

"Why the hell did you have to bring him here?"

"She had no choice," Hall told him.

"Get out."

"Not until we've talked." Hall caught hold of a chair, steadied himself.

"Someone," Greg said in a tone of deep satisfaction, "seems to have given you a real working over, and this time I wouldn't have lifted a hand to stop it."

"Welford didn't send a deputy. He came himself." The room tilted, steadied again.

Gail caught his arm, eased him into a chair. "Let him rest for a while. Can't you see he's at the end of his rope?"

"What difference —" Greg looked at his sister. "Oh!" The exclamation was jolted out of him. "Oh, hell! So that's it. I should have guessed, the way you've been carrying on." He went out of the room, came back with a glass which he shoved into Hall's hand. "Drink it!" He closed Hall's lax fingers around the glass, guided it to his mouth.

The brandy was smooth and strong. The first sip burned. The second cleared his head. His hand gripped the glass and he emptied it in three long swallows.

"Thanks. I needed that. For the last few days I've been punch-drunk."

Greg went out to mix highballs for Gail and himself. He came back to find his sister mopping up his spilled drink and Hall looking at the photograph of him with his wife.

"You know about Martha?" he asked harshly.

"Harry told me this afternoon."

"Harry?" Greg looked in puzzlement from Gail's face to Hall's.

201

"The garage man who repaired Robin's car after the —"

"You mean after he ran down my wife and killed her."

At the sound of Greg's voice Gail's hand closed convulsively on the arm of her chair.

"Yes," Hall said quietly. "That's what I meant. A tragic accident."

"He drove off." Greg's voice was shaking. "He just — left her there."

"But Hall didn't do that!" Gail said fiercely. "He's not responsible. Do you have to torture him?"

"We're all responsible." Hall sounded unutterably tired. "The more I see of this thing the more I realize we're all the killers, all the killed."

"Baloney!" Greg said rudely. "Spare me the phony philosophy and the 'No man is an island' stuff. Will that bring Martha back?"

"What will? Even if Robin had faced his responsibility, would it have mattered? Except to him. He was the one who had to live with it." Before Greg could answer he asked, "What happened the day you took Lillian to lunch at the Stagecoach?"

Gail threw out a hand in warning but Greg ignored it.

"She called me. She sounded nuts. I couldn't make head or tail of what she was getting at.

Finally she asked me to meet her at the Stagecoach for lunch so we could talk."

He had seen her around the village, of course. Everyone knew the Halsteds and after her marriage to the great war hero she was noticed wherever she went. Just a pretty kid with bright hair and a kind of sunniness. No clouds in her sky. Martha had met her somewhere. Said she was enchanting, like something out of a fairy tale, all sparkle. Only what happened to people like that, she had wondered, if they ever had to face reality? Lillian was accustomed to having her own way; she accepted it without arrogance but as a kind of divine right. But the day came, usually, when people had to grow up, to realize that something they wanted was forever out of their reach and to accept it with a good grace.

Since Martha's death Greg had just gone through the motions. Her loss was a constant heavy ache. Her accidental death had grown in his mind to cold-blooded murder and the hatred this engendered helped to ease his pain, at least to sidetrack it from time to time. And by hating the unknown who had killed her he was able to forget that if he had not taken the car that day she would not have been walking.

The frantic telephone call from Lillian Masson had bewildered him. Gone off her rocker, he had thought, and he hadn't liked the idea of meeting her for lunch. What did the girl want of him?

That day the Stagecoach had been bursting at the seams and if it hadn't been for Lillian's insistence they would never have got a table, certainly not one that was as remote as possible from the center of activity swirling around the Connecticut Mussolini, Millard Welford.

The girl had been tense and she had stared at him as though he had left his other head at home.

"Mr. Carlyle," she had said as soon as the harried waiter had taken their orders and gone, "I know Robin killed your wife but he can't pay you any more. He simply can't. He didn't mean to do it. He couldn't help it. Please give us time. We know you have a right to it. All we ask is time. Please!"

"What in the world," Greg had asked, "are you talking about?"

"That forty thousand dollars. We can't raise it. Not just now."

"I never heard —"

"Oh, please. Please." She had begun to cry and it was as embarrassing as hell. For a moment Greg considered clearing out of there in a hurry. The girl should be locked up.

"I never knew until this morning," she said. "Then he — Robin got your last blackmail note and he told me the whole thing. I don't blame you, Mr. Carlyle. Neither of us blames you. Robin says your wife just stepped out from behind a parked car and fell right in front of his wheels and he couldn't stop in time."

The tears were spilling down her cheeks and she brushed them away with an oddly childlike gesture as though unaware of what she was doing.

"He panicked, I guess. He lost his head. He had seen so much death, so much — so he drove away from it. We'll give you everything we have, only we need time. Just a little time."

So Gregory Carlyle knew at last who had killed his wife. "And that girl sat there," he said, "accusing me of blackmail! No one had ever identified the hit-run driver. I had no idea who he was. Just some cowardly bastard who got away with it. And on top of finding Martha's murderer I am accused of blackmail! I told her I hadn't even known who had killed my wife until she told me. I told her I didn't want their damned money. I'd never had Martha appraised. I told her I'd strip her lousy, yellow husband of his medals and tear down that obelisk with my own hands."

"And then?" Hall said quietly.

"And then," Greg's voice was dull, his hatred exhausted, "she said, 'I can't give you back your wife. But if that's what you want, I'll pay your debt.' And she ran out of the place, crying aloud like a small child."

"And later," Hall said, "she went to the library to see Gail."

"Can't we keep Gail out of this?" Greg asked.

"You know we can't. What happened, Gail?"

"She was crying. She wanted Greg to wait a few days or a few weeks, something to give her time. I didn't understand what it was all about. And then she told me her husband had been the hit-run driver who killed Martha."

"That's what scared Gail," Greg said. "She was afraid you'd think it gave me a motive for killing them. That's why she tried to — sidetrack you. At least in the beginning."

Gail interrupted her brother hastily. "Greg didn't kill them, Hall. He didn't."

"Did Lillian write you a letter?"

Greg shook his head. "That one meeting was the only personal contact I ever had with either of them."

"So I'm back where I started," Hall said at last.

"Who killed Cocky Robin?" Greg added shame-facedly. "Sorry. That was out of line."

"If it's vengeance you want, Carlyle, Robin

suffered. Welford used him. Harry Wilkes bled him white. And that obelisk tortured him. Burgess was right when he said that Robin was glad to die. But I still don't know who killed him and who killed Lillian."

After a long time Greg said, "You know, at the time I didn't care enough, one way or the other, to wonder about it. Not until you came back and Gail began to worry. So far as we both could see, I was the only one who had a motive. How about a drink? Bourbon? Martini?"

Hall hid his surprise. "A martini would be fine."

"Gail, can't you scrape up something to eat?" Greg met Hall's eyes and grinned sheepishly. "We might as well learn to get along together."

"Just as well," Hall agreed.

"You — you two —" Gail went out of the room quickly, her color high.

"She's the hell of a nice girl if she is my sister," Greg said.

"I'm aware of that. I thought I had already made myself clear on that point."

"I didn't realize then that it was mutual — that is —"

"Greg," Gail called from the kitchen, "are you or are you not going to fix drinks?"

"Coming."

"And no talking behind my back. Either of you."

In commiseration Greg shook his head at Hall. "What a life you are letting yourself in for."

Rather dubiously Hall held out his hand and the other man took it.

III

Dinner was a silent affair. All three were deep in their own thoughts. Hall was brooding. Greg was somber. Gail busied herself with serving and did not look up.

Only when the dishes had been cleared away did Greg say, "Let's get on with it, shall we? You were right about one thing. There's no peace for any of us until this thing is cleared up." He looked at Hall. "Where do we start?"

"Back at the beginning. No, not quite the beginning. We've learned everything, in a way, except — who killed them. We know that the death of your wife triggered everything that has happened since. Harry realized, when Robin brought in his car for repairs, that he was the hit-run driver. There must have been — traces."

Hall looked down at his hands and Greg looked at nothing at all.

"So Harry blackmailed Robin for money to

establish himself in the community as a man of substance. It's funny in a way. But no stranger than the extraordinary devices to which some perfectly respectable women will resort to give their children what they call a fair chance. Robin, of course, never dreamed that it was Harry who was getting the money. He assumed that it was you, the man whose wife he had killed, who was the blackmailer. That is undoubtedly why he paid without protest. He thought it was a kind of debt.

"Meanwhile, Harry got drunk and talked too much, or too little, to Millard Welford, who lacked local prestige in building his neofascist party. Welford assumed, from Harry's hints, that Lillian was having an affair with you. So he mentioned your name in a knowing sort of way and Robin consented to back him.

"I am not," Hall went on painfully, "trying to justify Robin. He had always been reckless but he had never been held responsible for his actions. I share the blame for that. I was older and I probably shielded him when I shouldn't have. But the time came when Welford put his gang into action and Robin, thank God, refused to swallow that.

"Then Harry made his final strike and Robin couldn't raise the money. He had to tell Lillian and she went to bat for him. Thank God for that, too. But that night she died."

209

After a long time Gail said, "Then you came home and the trouble started."

"The trouble started," Hall agreed. "No one wanted the case opened up. Welford had one of his boys send me an anonymous letter warning me off; had my tires slashed; had me roughed up; and finally burned down my house, thinking I still had that set of instructions. And that, incidentally, is going to stop him in his tracks. Then today he damned near finished the job. But he's single-minded. He didn't want anything discovered that would hurt Robin's prestige because he had to have it. I don't believe he killed them."

"What about Harry Wilkes?" Greg asked.

"Oh, he got the money. He blackmailed Robin. But he's not a killer. He's just a hometown boy trying to make good by the only method he knows."

"So what's left?"

"Lillian mailed a letter a few minutes before she died. If I could find out who got that letter I think I'd have the answer."

"Have you asked the Halsteds?"

"Her uncle was so angry with her — and Lillian with him —" Hall broke off. "Halsted hated the marriage. He told me so. He's been as queer as hell about the whole thing. He ordered me out of the house because I suggested Lillian might be involved. He tried to make me believe that Robin had killed them both, that there was no outside murderer."

"But what happened to the missing weapon?" Greg asked. "That came out at the investigation. There has to be an outside killer."

"Halsted buried it in his rose garden." Hall stood up.

"Where are you going?" Gail asked sharply.

"I'm going to look for that gun."

"But why would Bruce Halsted — ?"

"That's what I'm going to find out. Where are those car keys, Gail?"

"I'll drive for you this time," Greg offered.

"We're all going," Gail declared firmly.

FOURTEEN

After all, they decided not to use the car for the single block to the top of the Green. Greg was equipped with a spade and Hall carried a flashlight, as though, Gail commented, they were prepared to bury the body.

The two men, with Gail between them, walked slowly, partly because of Hall's condition, partly because they were unsure of what they were going to do. You can't, as Greg had pointed out, rough up an old man just because he refuses to talk.

There were lights in most of the houses and street lamps burned on the Green but there was no traffic. Their footsteps sounded loud in the quiet night.

"Though what the gun would prove I don't know, even if we found it," Greg said, thinking aloud. "Why did the old man hide it?"

"He said Robin had shot Lillian and then killed himself, that he wanted to protect their reputations from scandal."

"The Halsteds adored that girl," Greg said. "I can't see them covering for the lieutenant if they believed he had killed her."

"I never put the slightest trust in that theory, not for a minute. And now that we know Lillian was prepared to back Robin the best she knew how, there's no conceivable motive. What I can't figure out is that three-hour interval between Lillian's death and Robin's."

"What's that?" Greg asked, startled, and Hall explained.

"But that makes no sense!"

"It has to."

"Doctors can't estimate the time of death as closely as all that. They aren't infallible."

The street lamp in front of the Williamses' was a white glare and instinctively the three tried to walk more quietly. In front of the Halsted house they paused uncertainly. Lights blazed out on the garden from the long windows of the music room where, in his more active social days, Halsted had hired some of the famous string quartets to entertain his guests. Tonight they were playing a recording of the great Schubert quintet. The lovely slow movement had just begun and for a few moments the three invaders stood motionless.

Then Greg said, his voice hushed, "We're the hell of a bunch of conspirators. Anyone passing on the Green can see us out here. And if that gun is in the rose bed how do we get it? They might as well have spotlighted the place."

The lights from the music room poured out on the garden, on the rose bed.

"I thought that house was air-conditioned," Gail said.

"It is, but Mr. Halsted is getting deaf and they keep the thing loud. Anyhow, you know how some stereo fanatics are. Someone said they aren't satisfied until they can hear the spit being shaken out of the tuba."

"What do we do?" Gail asked. "Wait for them to go to bed?"

"You go home," Hall told her. "I'm going to take a chance. They may not even look out of the window."

Gail ignored him and went toward the rose bed, the two men following her. It was circular, perhaps thirty feet in diameter, with gravel paths, the bushes well spaced.

"Nothing but the best," Greg commented. "Though why would he put the gun here? He has a couple of gardeners, hasn't he?"

"Maybe the roses are his special province. Anyhow —"

"Anyhow," Greg said, "it looks to me as though the bushes had all had a lot of work done around them, which is a good way of concealing a special place, of course. Do we start at the beginning and go on to the end or what?"

"It would take all night." Gail protested.

"There are dozens of rose bushes. Dozens and dozens."

Hall stood looking at the circular rose bed. "Let's let our heads save our backs." Inside the big house there was the faint shrilling of a telephone. "There's something in my mind."

"That's nice to know," Gail commented.

"Quiet, wench. I'm thinking. Halsted took a prize with one of the roses, something he'd developed by grafting or however they do it. A white rose with streaks of pink. Something like that."

He turned the flashlight on one of the bushes, went on to another. Halfway round the circle he gave a triumphant exclamation and squatted down, grunting from the strain on sore muscles.

"I'm pretty sure this is the one."

"Does the ground look disturbed?" Greg asked.

"I'm no gardener but I suppose we'll have to find out."

"Okay, move out of the way but keep the light on it. I'll do the spade work."

Somewhere in the distance there was a siren that screamed once and then was stilled. There was no other sound but the grating of the spade on hidden pebbles. Even Bruce Halsted couldn't eliminate all the stones in the

Connecticut soil. Inside the house the quintet had begun the third movement of the Schubert.

Over and over Greg drove the spade into the ground. Then he stopped.

"Hit something. May be another rock. Give them a year and they grow into boulders. Or it may be what we are looking for."

Carefully he shoveled the soil to one side. Then he reached down, scraped away earth, brought up a revolver, his finger in the barrel, trying not to touch the grip.

"Well, here it is, and now what do we do with the damned thing?" Greg's startled face was caught in the beam of a powerful flashlight.

"You turn it over to me," Captain Gerfind said affably. The flashlight swept over Gail and Hall. "Oh, God! You again. I might have known. When there's trouble in Shelton, just look for Masson."

He took the revolver from Greg, handling it carefully, turned it over to the trooper behind him.

"And what's this all about?"

"That," Hall told him, "is the missing gun that killed my brother and his wife."

Gerfind said, with an effort at control, "Do you usually look for guns under rose bushes?"

"Mr. Halsted told me he had hidden it in the rose bed."

This time the captain was reduced to speechlessness.

"And, come to that, since when have you been patrolling rose bushes, Captain?"

"Mrs. Williams, who is fast becoming my favorite witness, saw people acting suspiciously on the Halsted grounds. She called Mr. Halsted who reported to us."

"Short and sweet," Hall said.

"But why would the old man hide the murder weapon?" Gerfind asked. "My God, the girl was his niece! Was he trying to protect her murderer?"

"That," Hall said patiently, "is what we came here tonight to find out."

"But Halsted!" The captain was aghast. "Shelton's leading citizen and all that. Say what you like about equality under the law but if I made a mistake about Halsted my head will be set on a pike in the Village Green."

"So?" There was a challenge in Hall's voice.

"Oh, it has to be done, of course," the captain said, and Hall grinned at him. "Come on and let's get it over with. But, my God, when you turn over a stone some damned thing always crawls out!"

"Better in the open than underground."

217

"Oh, sure. Sure. That is," Gerfind added dubiously, "I guess so."

II

Halsted opened the door. "Good evening, Captain. Thank you for being so prompt. Did you find —" He broke off as Captain Gerfind stepped aside to let Gail, Gregory, and Hall precede him. The trooper brought up the rear, holding carefully a dirt-encrusted revolver. Halsted stared at it as though he had been transfixed. Then, moving heavily, he led the way into the music room, where the Schubert was coming to an end.

"Harriet," he began helplessly.

Hall observed again the way in which Halsted's colorless little wife managed to take charge of a situation, however unprepared she might be. She came forward now, head high, manner gracious, smiling questioningly at Gail.

"I am Gail Carlyle, Mrs. Halsted."

"Oh, of course. The girl with the pretty voice who was so thoughtful in telling me about Hall's accident."

"And my brother Gregory."

"Mr. Carlyle. Do sit down, all of you." She was bewildered but gallant, the social disciplines of a lifetime serving her in good stead.

With an effort she turned to Hall. "Did you
— My dear boy! What has happened to you?"

"Nothing serious. I got tangled up in a
scrap."

"It's a way he has," Gerfind remarked ge-
nially.

Something about Halsted's frozen silence
after he had seen the gun and Mrs. Halsted's
determined graciousness in the face of the in-
vasion seemed to have given the policeman
more confidence. Masson had managed to hit
the nail on the head again. Halsted, unbeliev-
able as it seemed, was up to his neck in the
Masson murders. He was staring out of the
window, his shoulders bowed as though they
bore a weight too heavy for him to support.

"Perhaps you'd all like something to drink,"
Mrs. Halsted suggested with false brightness
when they were seated. She was endeavoring
to turn this unlikely situation into a social occasion.

Gerfind stopped her with a gesture. "Thank
you, no. What we would like is some information." He waited until Halsted had turned
back from the window. "Why did you bury
this gun, sir?"

Halsted looked at Hall. "I should have
known that you couldn't be trusted. You look
more reliable but you're like Robin, after all."

"Bruce!" his wife said warningly.

"You concealed vital evidence in a murder case, Mr. Halsted." The captain spoke without emphasis. "This is a serious matter. It makes you an accessory."

"No!"

Halsted moved beside his wife's chair, put his hand on her shoulder, more as though he were seeking comfort than providing it. "It has to come out, Harriet. I did it for the best." Again his tired eyes swept over Hall's battered face. "To shield your brother, to protect him. For Lillian's sake, because she loved him. But you had to come blundering around, to force this situation, to show up your brother for what he was."

"Let's get back to that gun, please," Gerfind said. "Does it belong to you?"

"Good God, no! I haven't handled a gun since World War I. It was Robin's. I found it —" His voice trailed off.

"Shall we take it from the beginning, sir?"

"Bruce is upset," his wife protested. "Some other time —"

Gerfind made no reply. He simply waited.

"That morning," Halsted said at last, "that morning — I've gone over all this with Hall. Is it necessary to do it again?"

"Mr. Masson," the captain commented dryly, "hasn't seen fit to confide in me."

"Well, Mrs. Cushing — that's the housekeeper — called to say she had found Lillian and Robin and they were both dead. She was almost incoherent with shock. I went over and found — and found —" After a moment he went on. "Mrs. Cushing had fainted beside the telephone. In the living room," he paused again, "Lillian was lying on the couch. She had been shot through the heart. Robin was on the floor with a bullet between his eyes. The gun was lying beside his hand."

Gerfind was staring at him in disbelief.

Halsted nodded grimly. "Murder and suicide. I — for Lillian's sake I pocketed the gun before I called you. There seemed no point — we couldn't bring them back or alter what had been done —" He gave a half groan and broke into harsh sobbing.

Mrs. Halsted had risen to put her arms around him, rocking him gently as though he were a child in pain. Gail looked away. There are emotions it is indecent to watch. She had never before seen a man cry. For a woman it brought relief as a rule but this seemed only to reveal an unbearable agony. Hall, she noticed, was watching Halsted with an odd expression on his face, as though something were happening behind the steady eyes. A growing comprehension mingled with horror.

"Know where he keeps his liquor?" Greg muttered and Hall led the way to the liquor cabinet in the big dining room. Greg splashed brandy in a glass and grinned at Hall. "This is getting to be a habit." The grin faded. "Do you think it could be true?"

Hall shook his head "It's not true and Halsted knows it's not true."

"Are you sure of that?"

"Virtually."

"You think you have it figured out?"

"I'm afraid so."

"Do you want to give the old man this brandy?"

"I am Halsted's least favorite character at this moment. He probably wouldn't accept a life preserver from me if he were going down for the third time."

The two young men returned to the music room to find that Halsted had regained his self-control. He and his wife were sitting side by side on a couch, holding hands. Halsted took the brandy Greg offered him.

"You've known from the beginning then," Gerfind said, "that the lieutenant murdered his wife and then committed suicide."

Halsted nodded.

"You usually get rumors in a village of this size. The Massons had a reputation for being unusually happy as a young couple. What went wrong?"

"The war, I suppose. In my day they called

it shell shock. I don't know what fancy name they have for it now. I didn't want Lillian to marry him. I told her that. But she," he controlled his working face muscles with a visible effort, "she had always been given her own way. She expected it. She didn't know how to — bend, to be flexible, when anything failed to go her way." His voice faded out.

"She was sweet," Mrs. Halsted said.

"Oh, yes, she was sweet. Why not? She always got what she wanted."

"Bruce!"

"You spoiled her, Harriet. We both spoiled her. A sweet little orphan and we had no young person to love, to take care of. Deny her nothing. That was our policy. We're responsible for what happened."

Again something flickered behind Hall's light eyes, and Gail found herself clenching her hands. Whatever it is, she thought, I don't want to know.

"Go on," Captain Gerfind said.

"You've had the story. There's nothing more to add."

"Motive, Mr. Halsted. Motive."

"I told you."

"If the lieutenant had suffered any kind of mental breakdown it would have showed up before now. To kill his wife, a girl he was madly in love with, and had been married to for only a few months — there has to be a hell of a reason."

There was something almost frenzied in Halsted's voice. "He shot her! It had to be that way."

"What had she done?"

"God damn it, she —" Halsted was shaking.

He couldn't take much more, Hall thought. The breaking point was near. Mrs. Halsted knew it too. She was paper white.

"Bruce! Bruce darling."

"Robin killed her," he repeated stubbornly. "There's no other answer. He had made a mess of things. Not worth the powder to blow up. I saw through that charming empty surface as soon as I laid eyes on him after the war. Then he got involved with Welford. Sat on platforms with him. Introduced him. Wonder to me he didn't wear a swastika or stand in front of a burning cross wearing a sheet."

Halsted forced himself to steady his voice. He pulled away from his wife's restraining hand.

Gerfind seemed willing to wait it out. It was Hall who asked, "Why did you quarrel with Lillian the day she died?"

Gerfind shook his head. How did the man do it? Pull things out of thin air like a conjurer? But this conjurer had something up his sleeve. The captain sensed it. He was prepared for

224

action but not the kind that followed. For the second time in her life Mrs. Halsted fainted.

III

Between them, Gail and the trooper lifted her onto the couch. Halsted, who had blustered, was useless and lost without his chief support.

At length Mrs. Halsted opened her eyes, looked around and said, "I'm sorry to make such a fuss." When Gail's hand pressed down on her shoulder she obeyed submissively and agreed to remain where she was. She summoned up a smile for her husband. "Silly of me. I'm all right now. Really I am."

"Then," Hall said, "let's get back to the question. Why did you quarrel with your niece, Mr. Halsted?"

Nothing will stop him, Gail thought. If Halsted had a heart attack Hall would simply wait. But sooner or later he would ask the question again.

"Robin was being blackmailed." Halsted looked around and found no surprise. "You all seem to have known. I didn't. Lillian telephoned that morning and asked to borrow forty thousand dollars. Cool as you please. No explanations. But I told her to come over here.

"At first she tried to lie about it, said she

needed the money for herself. Then she told me Robin had been blackmailed. He had had a letter that morning demanding a final payment of forty thousand, which had to be made by the Fourth of July, just five days off. He couldn't raise it. He had already paid out thirty thousand and there were no more funds available until he could sell some real estate. And he couldn't wait. She refused to tell me what it was all about. She just kept saying she loved Robin and he hadn't been to blame.

"Well, I've never knuckled down to pressure and I didn't then. I said I wouldn't fall for any blackmail. She — we were both angry. She went home."

"Screaming out, 'You'll be sorry,' " Hall said.

There was only defeat in Halsted's face. Gail hoped that Hall would let the old man alone. Of course, he didn't.

"What was in that letter she wrote you, Mr. Halsted?"

"She didn't mean it! God, she didn't mean it! Robin killed her!"

"Where is the letter?"

Halsted stood up, weaving on his feet, and stumbled out of the room. At a gesture from Gerfind the trooper followed him. The silence in the room was unbroken until they returned. Halsted held out a crumpled envelope to Hall

226

and sat down, shielding his eyes with a shaking hand.

Hall pulled out the letter, read it quickly. He caught his breath but his voice was steady. "That's the only way it could have happened."

The captain reached for the letter, Halsted made an instinctive gesture of protest, and then his hand dropped.

"You might as well read it aloud, Hall," he said wearily.

Hall read, his voice flat, without expression:

"Everything in the world has given way. First the Welford man tried to force Robin to do something wrong. Then the blackmailer said he would destroy Robin. I thought you would help but you won't. Now there is only one way left. I said I'd pay his debt. A wife for a wife. Now maybe he'll be satisfied and let Robin alone. So I'm going to shoot myself and the score will be even. I told you that you'd be sorry."

The curiously childish, vindictive note of the spoiled girl sounded odd on Hall's lips.

"Oh, thank God!" Mrs. Halsted's exclamation shocked them all. "I was so afraid. I had never seen Bruce so angry. And I saw him bring home that gun and bury it —"

"God!" Greg headed out of the room, the door of the first-floor lavatory slammed shut.

"I'm sorry," Hall said at last, "but I had

to know. Mrs. Halsted had to know, because she believed her husband was a murderer."

"I might as well have been," Halsted said. "I was responsible. I've tried desperately to make myself believe she didn't mean it, that Robin had killed her. But I was responsible."

"We were all responsible." Greg, looking white and sick, had returned to the room. "Let's get the hell out of here."

FIFTEEN

Captain Gerfind made no objection to their leaving. There were two dark silhouettes standing at an upstairs window of the Williams house. Mrs. Williams's cup must be overflowing, Hall thought. He wondered what she made of the spade Greg was carrying.

Before they passed the Williams house the police car went by. Whatever further ordeal Halsted might have to undergo, the captain had been merciful enough to provide a respite.

They parted at the corner without words, the Carlyles going down the Green, Hall continuing along Elm Street toward the sprawling, old-fashioned house where Burgess lived.

The lights were on and the door wide open, the screen unlocked. The house was empty. The old man must be wandering again, trying to fill a sleepless night.

Hall switched out the lights and sat on a battered old rocking chair on the screened porch, looking into the darkness. Somewhere a baby wailed fretfully and then was still. A prowling cat drifted down the street.

From here there was no view of the obelisk,

for which Hall was grateful. He knew now how Robin had spent the hours between Lillian's suicide and his own death. Glad to die? God, yes! He would have run with open arms to meet death when life was stripped of everything he valued, and his small, bright-haired bride lay dead by her own hand in an effort to protect him. Or to punish her uncle because he had, inexplicably, failed her?

And yet people forget. In the long run the poignant tragedies, the great triumphs, all become equally dim. Worse than that, they become unimportant. In time Robin would have found life sweet again. Not so bright and shining, perhaps, but good enough. That was more than most people got.

A dog barked once and then stopped. It ran out to greet the frail, stooped figure that walked slowly down the street. Burgess bent to pat its head. Then he came up on the porch, opened the screen door.

"You are late tonight," Hall said from the darkened porch.

"You're still up, Hall?" The old man settled himself in the other rocking chair. "This is pleasant. It's a long time since I've found anyone waiting for me when I came home." The rocker moved backward and forward, creaking over a loose floorboard.

"When on earth do you sleep?" Hall asked.

"I don't need much sleep any more, and walking helps. Of course it's more difficult during the winter months. Always afraid I'll slip. What would I do if I broke a hip? Horrible to be laid up. And there's no one really to carry on my work."

"It means a lot to you, doesn't it?"

"It's useful work, Hall. I know a lot of people think it's nonsense to try to set these youngsters on the right path."

"How can anyone decide what's the right path?"

"Between right and wrong, there's no question at all. The choice is always there."

"But your right might be my wrong."

The rocking chair moved rhythmically. "It takes a certain maturity to make one understand that under all the apparent chaos there's a single clear pattern."

"And you want to establish that pattern."

"Not for my sake, Hall. Mine is a very humble part. To keep others from going astray. To prevent men like Welford from setting up —"

"A different pattern?"

"I don't understand you tonight, Hall. Surely you can't approve of Welford's system."

"I abominate it. But I am just as opposed to any system that is imposed on me."

"But otherwise we have chaos."

"There's something called freedom of choice," Hall pointed out. "You said once that the end justifies the means. How far did you mean that?"

The chair creaked back and forth. "It's an imperfect world," the old man said in his gentle voice.

" 'O cursed spite, That ever I was born to set it right.' But you aren't as indecisive as Hamlet, are you? When you find it necessary, you act."

The rocking chair was still now. "When I find it necessary," Burgess said at last. "After all, one can't live merely with one's theories; one must put them into effect."

There was no change in Hall's voice. "Why was it necessary for you to kill Robin?"

II

"Shall we go inside?" Burgess said at last. "The night air is rather chilly."

In the living room he moved with sure feet among the crowded pieces of furniture, switching on the Tiffany lamps, closing windows. His face wore a pinched look as though he were very cold.

Hall went into the kitchen where he boiled water, dropped a bouillon cube in a cup, dissolved it, and opened a can of beer for himself. He came back to give the old man the hot drink and tilted back his beer can.

"This is thoughtful of you," Burgess said, and he sipped cautiously at the scalding drink. "Now why did you leap to that extraordinary conclusion?"

"I didn't," Hall admitted. "I just kept stumbling over pieces I couldn't fit into the puzzle. It wasn't until the last one fell into place that I knew. Everything except — why?"

"My dear boy!" Burgess was amused. "Do I look like a killer?"

"The most vicious-looking man I ever saw was a quiet but enthusiastic music dealer with violent opinions. Violent opinions and gentle behavior can, after all, go together."

"So. What was it then?"

"The night prowling, for one thing. It could put you on the right spot at the right time. The determination to guide your boys in your way. Your contention that the end justifies the means. Your — unforgivingness. Your fear of Welford."

"Hall, you didn't see the riot Welford stirred up. It was unspeakable. He was turning good boys into mindless tools. And Robin — Welford could not have accomplished anything without Robin's support."

"But Robin had refused to go on with it.

Welford had lost his backing, which was a lot more harmful than never having had it at all."

"I wish I could let you continue to believe that," Burgess said. "But Robin didn't change for the better at the end. He changed for the worse." He finished drinking the bouillon and set the cup down carefully on its saucer.

"I haven't been sleeping," he said, when Hall had waited for a long time. "Night after night, I remembered the Hitler horrors, thought how that obscene growth, under a variety of names, was beginning to attack the whole political body again. It was wrong and it had to be stopped. I'm afraid," he added apologetically, "I rather lost my detachment. I knew Robin was the key figure. I was walking and happened to pass his house that night. It was very late but the lights were still on. No car was parked in front so I assumed they were still up but that they had no guests. It occurred to me that I might be able to reason with Robin, make him see the disaster he could bring to his community by sponsoring the forces that deal in hate, how he could tarnish his reputation."

He was silent for a long while, remembering. He had rung the bell but there was no answer. Then he had tried the door. It was unlocked and swung open at his touch. Lillian lay on a couch, shot to death, the revolver on the floor beside her. Robin sat slumped in a chair, staring at nothing.

"I must have cried out. He didn't even move. Then I went to him, shook his shoulder. I said, 'What have you done?' And he looked up but without seeming to focus. I don't believe he even recognized me. He had gone very far into the hell of his own making that night. And I said, 'Are you responsible for this?' And Robin said, his mouth loose as though he couldn't control it, 'Yes, I am to blame.'

"I knew then that there was only one way. There is no turning back from murder; and with his popularity and charm, he could get away with it. So I picked up the gun. He knew what I intended to do, I think, for suddenly he smiled. He had a shining sort of smile, you know. And he said, 'Why not?' So I shot him and came away."

Burgess added, "I told you in the beginning, and it's the truth, Hall, if that comforts you. Robin was glad to die."

After a while Hall went out to the kitchen and poured himself a stiff drink. When he returned Burgess looked at him anxiously. "You are exhausted. You've been doing too much and had too many shocks. Don't you think you ought to get some rest?"

For a moment, Hall was shaken by a convulsive impulse to laugh. "Not yet. Not just yet. There are still a few threads to untangle, aren't there?"

Burgess frowned and then his face cleared. "Of course," he agreed. "The law demands its eye for an eye, doesn't it? You'll want to call the State Police." He pushed the telephone across the table within Hall's reach. "But it's really a pity, in a way. I've been doing quite useful work."

"But you've lost your historical perspective, haven't you? And your research discipline. You've forgotten to build a structure on proven fact, not on theory. You didn't check your evidence."

This upset Burgess more than the accusation of murder. "I saw Lillian's dead body. I saw the gun. I saw Robin's face with everything wiped out of it. I heard his confession. There was no possible mistake."

"She left a letter for her uncle," Hall told him, "explaining that Robin had become involved with Welford; that he was being blackmailed; that she was going to kill herself in order to remove the blackmailer's hold, or rather to cancel it out."

Realization grew in the old man's face. "Then she shot herself! But I meant it for the best." He got out of his chair. "I'll just

236

straighten up some papers in my study so you can go to bed." He gave the telephone another push in Hall's direction and went out of the room.

Hall made no move to reach the telephone. The job he had set himself was finished.

In a little while Burgess came back. "I think I'll go for a short walk. I won't disturb you when I come back. Good night, Hall."

Hall made no move to stop him. He heard the old man's uncertain feet go down the steps, heard them echo on the sidewalk. Before going to bed he locked the door. Burgess would not be coming back again.

III

Oddly enough, he slept. The jangle of the telephone awakened him. It must, he thought, be very early. The room was dark. Then he heard the rush of rain and realized that the long drought had been broken at last.

He went into the living room to answer the telephone and saw by the tall clock against the wall that it was after ten. He had, after all, slept almost six hours.

"Hall!"

"Hello, Gail."

"Have you heard?"

"Heard what?" I wonder how he managed

it, Hall thought.

"Poor old Mr. Burgess. He must have fallen in the river. They found him this morning."

The easiest way out, Hall thought. And quick. It must have been fairly quick. He hoped it had been.

"Hall! Did you hear me? Didn't you notice he hadn't come home?"

"I didn't expect him to come home."

"You — why?"

"He shot and killed Robin. He told me last night."

"No, not Mr. Burgess! The gentlest man."

"But ruthless, as you mentioned once before, when he believed that he was right."

"But why?"

"He went to the house that night to talk to Robin and saw Lillian lying dead. He jumped to the conclusion that Robin had killed her. So, in the line of duty, he executed him." After a pause Hall said, "He told me that he had meant it for the best."

"Oh, Hall! The poor old man. Did you tell him he was mistaken?"

"Yes, I told him. He went out, leaving me to call the police."

"But you didn't?"

"No, I didn't."

"Then you thought he'd take this way out?"

"Well —"

"Hall, bless you!"

"Does that mean I'm forgiven? I've built up quite a score with you: bullying, inciting to crime, involving you in gang wars, misjudging your brother."

"Greg was so shaken by Lillian's suicide that he walked the floor most of the night. He kept saying, 'A wife for a wife.' He was just about out of his mind, thinking he had driven her to it. Thank God, it's Sunday and he can sleep."

"But you're awake and so am I," he pointed out.

"Well —"

"The police will probably be calling here and I don't want you mixed up in anything else."

"I make good waffles," she suggested.

"I eat good waffles."

"Then come around. Anyhow, I've got something to show you."

"What's that?" He was instantly suspicious.

She laughed. "Wait and see."

"Good or bad?"

"The best," she assured him.

When he had shaved and showered, looking in disbelief at his face because he hadn't known it was possible for human flesh to display so many varieties of color, like an off-focus sunset on color television, he dressed in record time. This was one appointment he wanted to keep without being chaperoned by the State Police.

Gail admitted him, wearing a big apron over her light dress. "Haven't you enough sense to wear a raincoat? For heaven's sake, come out to the kitchen. You're dripping all over the rug."

"That is not the kind of welcome a man likes to get from his heart's delight. House-proud women scare hell out of me. There are a few questions I've got to ask before I'm permanently committed. Do you rush around shoving ashtrays under cigarettes? Do you want your husband to spend his weekends repairing the faucet? Do you —" He checked the light tone he had adopted, leaned forward to kiss her. "I don't dare come closer. I'll get that pretty dress wet."

"It washes."

After a somewhat tumultuous interlude she said in a tone of wonder, "And all that before you've even had a cup of coffee! What kind of man am I getting?"

"A prize," he assured her, "but speaking of coffee —"

He sat at the kitchen table in shirt sleeves, his wet coat dripping from a hanger, drinking coffee while she mixed waffles and turned sausages in the pan.

"A very domestic scene," Greg remarked as he came into the kitchen. "American small-town Sunday at its most typical. All we need are the funny papers."

"Papers!" Gail exclaimed. "That's the other thing I had to tell you, Hall."

"The other thing?" Greg looked from one revealing face to the other, his eyes mocking.

By tacit consent Hall and Gail agreed to postpone the news of Burgess's death until after breakfast.

"Greg, get the paper, will you?"

"She orders people around," Greg informed Hall. "It's a dog's life." He brushed past the wet coat. "Neither rain nor hail," he commented, "stop him on his appointed round. He comes here like a homing pigeon. Man, are you hooked!" He went to the living room, came back with the great mass of the Sunday paper.

"Look at the second section," Gail told him.

Greg went through the automatic task of separating the various sections of the paper, the sheep from the goats. Then he looked at the second section, skimming headlines; he began to read. Slowly a grin split his face. He passed on the paper. The headline seemed to leap off the page:

FASCIST TECHNIQUES EXPOSED

241

"You know what," Greg commented as he buttered a waffle lavishly, poured syrup on it, "I'll bet Welford's appetite is ruined this morning."

SIXTEEN

Captain Gerfind let Gail refill his cup with coffee. His eyes had hardly left Hall's face during his long detailed account.

"Why didn't you try to stop the old man or at least call the police?"

"Mr. Burgess was not attempting to escape his punishment. If he preferred to inflict it on himself —" Hall went on bitterly, "Surely the cause of justice has been served."

Gerfind, stirring his coffee absorbedly, made no reply.

"I came here to run down Robin's killer," Hall went on, "like one of the Furies, as Mrs. Halsted pointed out. Their function, as you may remember, was to pursue and punish sinners. What I found was — well, look at it for yourself. Burgess shot Robin because he believed he had killed Lillian and that he would continue to back Welford. He meant it for the best.

"Lillian shot herself because she thought it would take Greg off Robin's back, though he had nothing to do with the situation, and also as a kind of childish and vindictive revenge on Halsted because, for the first time in her life, she couldn't have her own way. She meant it for the best, too.

"Halsted refused to pay a blackmailer and then believed he was responsible for Lillian's suicide. He meant it for the best but he couldn't face the consequences and he hid that gun so it would appear to be a double murder.

"Harry blackmailed Robin because he wanted money to make himself a substantial citizen, which, incidentally, he will probably become. He saved my life at considerable risk when he'd have been a hell of a lot safer and better off if he had let me burn to death.

"Welford used Robin because he wanted, genuinely, I think, to save the world."

Hall was drawing meaningless patterns on the table with a forefinger.

"Robin had run down Mrs. Carlyle. Apparently she fell in front of his car and he couldn't stop in time to save her. Of course he should have stayed there to face his responsibility but he didn't. I'd helped as much as anyone else to shield Robin from his responsibilities, so I can't clear myself of blame. And out of that tragic accident came the blackmail, the involvement with Welford, Lillian's suicide, Robin's murder."

Hall looked at Gerfind. "So who is to blame, Captain? Yesterday I discovered that

I'm a potential killer, too. I came so close to strangling Welford —" He shook his head. "I'm no longer in a position to pass judgment."

"But someone has to," Gerfind said. "We can't all just pass the buck."

"A jury of our peers?"

"That's the law and I didn't make the law. Anyhow, I don't see a better one."

"Of course, you can report that Burgess shot Robin, thinking he had killed his wife. You can report that Lillian shot herself thinking Greg was blackmailing Robin. You can report that Halsted concealed evidence in a murder case because he held himself responsible for driving his niece to her death. They all meant it for the best. Wrong? Of course they were wrong. But where's the justice, man?"

Captain Gerfind looked from the intent faces of the two Carlyles to Hall's battered and exhausted one.

"I suppose," he said, "this might be called a jury of their peers."

"Not guilty," Gail said.

"Not guilty," Greg echoed.

Now they were watching the captain. "It gives us a black eye," he said, "to have an unsolved murder in this place. But — I'd like that obelisk to stand. Say what you like, people need their heroes. It gives them something to measure up to. However," and his manner became brisk, "we've got some other problems. Harry Wilkes and his blackmail, for instance."

"He saved my life," Hall reminded him.

"Blackmail is a filthy thing and we can't let him think he can get away with it."

"Suppose," Hall suggested, "we get a full confession from him and a written agreement that he'll pay the money back, say at five thousand a year, with you as witness, and the statement to be kept at the barracks."

"My God!" Gerfind exclaimed in horror. "I'd be on record as conniving at a crime." He lighted a cigarette. "I suppose I could keep it at home," he said at last.

"And Welford?"

"You saw the paper?" Gerfind grinned. "We intended to haul him in this morning for arson, providing incendiary bombs, inciting to riot, and setting his gang on you."

"Intended to?"

"He and his wife have cleared out. Left for parts unknown. And no chance to take his money with him. His party is dead as the dodo. Probably, sooner or later, he'll start over somewhere, under another name, but he'll be starting from scratch. He'll never dare try to get his money, and it's a cinch his backers will have no further use for him. In fact, they may prefer to — eliminate him altogether. If they don't get him, the insurance investigators will. On the whole, I think I'd rather have taken my medicine and a prison term. It's safer that way."

"You know," Greg confessed at last, "I feel let down. As though the villains should be dragged screaming to justice."

"They've had it," Hall said. "For God's sake, can't we ever choose the peaceful way?"

"That's our only hope of survival," Gail said.

Captain Gerfind stood up. "We'll talk to Harry tomorrow. He's been giving those boys of his hell. I wouldn't be surprised if he managed to straighten some of them out in time." He held out his hand. "You're quite a guy, Masson. I wish we had more like you in Shelton. Are you planning to stay?"

"I have to go back to Egypt for at least a few days to finish up and then I'll be busy preparing for a lecture tour across the country."

"Do I or do I not fit into this restless future of yours?" Gail demanded.

He looked at her in astonishment. "But you are my future."

Greg laughed. "Shouldn't there, at least, be

a fadeout with the sun breaking through the clouds?"

"We needed the rain to clear the air," the captain reminded him. "It's been a long hot summer."

q. 10-11